Serai
William DeFoore PhD
used book $ 2.75

SERAI

Bringing the Children Home

By William Gray DeFoore, Ph.D.

WingSpan Press

Printed in the United States of America

Published by WingSpan Press, Livermore, CA
www.wingspanpress.com

The WingSpan name, logo and colophon are the trademarks of WingSpan Publishing.

ISBN 978-1-59594-131-2

First edition 2007

Library of Congress Control Number 2007923471

ACKNOWLEDGMENTS

I am deeply grateful to my wonderful wife Cindy for her editing, support and encouragement in the final stages of preparing Serai for publication. Her eye for detail and ability to see things that I don't has been a hugely valuable asset. I also want to thank all of the human beings who have bared their souls to me over the fifty-eight years of my life. This along with my own personal self-discovery process has revealed the amazing tapestry of our collective humanity, which you will find represented in *Serai*. And finally, I want to acknowledge my animal friends, who have spoken to me in their own language of the wild beauty that resides within the soul of every inhabitant of planet Earth.

Appreciation also goes to Jim Matterer of GodeCookery.com, who was kind enough to allow me to use the beautiful woodcut art you will find throughout this book.

TABLE OF CONTENTS

INTRODUCTION

This book has been evolving over a period of fourteen years. The story is designed to guide you, the reader, on a journey of self-discovery in which you ultimately recognize your own magnificence. The characters, the plot and the drama are a direct outgrowth of my personal and professional experience regarding emotional healing and transformation.

Drawing on the work of Carl Jung, Joseph Campbell, Marion Woodman, John Matthews, Clarissa Pinkola Estes, Thomas Moore and Robert Bly, to name but a few, the mythology underlying the story of Serai is in some ways familiar and in many ways unique. The uniqueness arises from my understanding of the psychological integration process and how it facilitates spiritual evolution.

The story can be seen as a roadmap to a deeper and more profound experience of personal fulfillment and joy. The three-part progression that John Matthews refers to as "Glory, Eclipse and Recovery" can easily be identified in the story of Serai as she appears, submerges into the shadows, and re-emerges in a surprisingly pervasive manner.

Each of the characters may be seen as representing the various aspects of your inner being. While you will find yourself identifying more strongly with some than with others, they will all have something to offer if you look deeply enough. Every character's journey, struggle and joyful celebration will show you possibilities for how you might find your own way to fulfillment.

It is my hope and prayer that this work will serve as a guide to those who choose to believe that life is precious in all its forms. The vision of Serai is one in which human beings are naturally, constantly evolving into wiser, more compassionate, magical beings whose inherent purpose is to bring joy and beauty into each moment.

Chapter One: The Castle Corazon

The light of day has faded on the castle Corazon, and a soft glow draws us to a minor courtyard at the rear of the castle keep. A small gathering of common folk huddle close around a glowing fire as the night creeps in. A tall, gaunt woman has so captured the group's attention that they don't seem to notice the frigid air.

Old Marguerite is a storehouse of age and wisdom. Something in her presence brings a sense of stillness and quiet to those who gather around. Sharp, high cheekbones and deep-set eyes define her craggy face, set off by a tangle of black and silver hair. Her sharp eyes, piercing with the slightest hint of mischief are enough to bring on a kind of trance before she utters a word.

As we move in a little closer, we can hear that she is weaving a story. Her listeners are still as statues as they hang on every word, mesmerized by the mysterious light dancing in the old woman's eyes.

Marguerite tells of a time long ago when...

The Castle Corazon was a sanctuary, where all of the children were cherished as innocent, creative beings of great value. They were free to laugh, to play and explore, yet their safety was closely guarded. In those days, peace and prosperity prevailed for all.

The sick, unsightly, wounded or strange of all ages were seen as aspects of the eternal child, and each had a place of value and comfort. All were accepted and honored exactly as they were, whoever or however they were.

The castle folk listened in silent awe, for their world was far different from the one the old woman described. Corazon was no longer a safe place. Not only the children were in danger of criticism and judgment, but now the infirm or unattractive of all ages were hidden from view lest they be chastised, condemned and persecuted.

The old woman continued her story.

In those days, none could remember a time when the feeling of compassion and deep connection did not exist between the weak and the strong, the old and the young, the beautiful and the plain, the rich and the poor. It was a time when everyone held an appreciation for all of life. This was reflected in the great care and sensitivity that was shown in all their actions.

The faces of those around the brazier seemed to glow as they imagined such a world of peace and harmony. Rich images unfolded slowly in their minds as Marguerite continued.

♥The Divine Serai

Though few spoke of it, there was among the children one pure and innocent child, divine in her radiant love for all. Her name was Serai, and she embodied the very heart of the castle. In a way no one could quite understand, her quiet powerful presence fueled the compassion and enthusiasm of all those in the realm.

Serai was not treated as if she was special or different from the other children, nor did she want to be. Her joy sprang from the simple act of living, and of being a part of the life and the community she loved. The sound of her laughter and the warmth of her smile brought peace and connection to the people of Corazon. All who were touched by Serai's presence were infused with her soft light, and it eased their suffering and gave new energy to their lives.

Even the animals and beasts of the field were honored in Corazon, and lived among the people as companions and allies. It was a common sight to see children and wild animals playing together in an open field, or chasing each other around the castle gardens. There was no fear, and safety was simply understood.

And then things in Corazon began to change.

The lord and lady of the castle had grown rich and powerful from years of prosperity. These conditions transformed them from within, and they actually started to believe that they were better and more important than those who served them. They became increasingly more demanding of their servants and underlings.

And they would no longer allow anything to continue that was displeasing to them.

"Those loud and unsightly children distract me from the events and affairs of the castle," Lord Peter remarked to Lady Delia as they passed a group of children playing near the castle keep. Some of the children were dirty from their play, and one had a deformed leg and ran with a noticeable wobble. Yet all of the children were exuberant in their frolic, shouting and laughing with total abandon.

"Is there not someone to care for them where they will be out of our sight? Surely we do not need to be exposed to such as this," Peter continued. "Are there not more like Serai? She is so beautiful and fair to look upon."

The elegant pair now focused on the small blond girl playing among the others, whose hair shone with such radiance that her head appeared to glow.

Lady Delia said nothing and nodded only slightly.

She had often had the same thoughts, but was reluctant to voice them to her husband. Now, hearing his words, she silently hoped that he would indeed make a change with regard to the unsightly ones—if it seemed to be his idea, he would be more likely to act on it.

Serai looked up from her play. She noticed the tone of Peter's words and the expressions of both adults as they passed, and a feeling of sadness swept over her.

As she watched the attractive couple walk away, Serai felt as much sorrow for them as for those they judged.

"Serai! It's your turn!" Her friend's voice brought the girl's attention back to her companions and their game of Fox and Geese, as Peter and Delia disappeared around a corner.

♥ The Disappearance of the Beasts and Children

And then, one by one, the animals were taken away.

Many of the wealthier castle dwellers had complained about the odors caused by the animals, and sometimes the larger of the beasts were just too frightening. Though the people and the animals had lived together for many years without mishap, the need for cleanliness, control and beautification created a growing distance between the two-legged and the four-legged residents of the castle.

Soon, most of the animals had been captured, caged, or sent away. The effects were subtle yet powerful.

A few months later while looking from the window of her living quarters in the quiet of an early morning, Delia had the brief thought, "I wonder where the lions are. They are usually roaming through the courtyard this time of day."

And then, "Ohh...now I remember." The Lady's shoulders dropped in despair at this moment, as she said softly to herself, "We sent them away."

Refusing to let herself feel the sorrow suddenly welling up in her heart, Delia turned from the window. Looking about her chambers in agitation and not knowing what else to do, she shouted impatiently for her maidservant, "Marie! Where is my breakfast?"

The next wave of change in Corazon swept away the crippled and poor of all ages, and any child deemed to be unpleasant or unattractive. The sight of castle guards rounding up small groups here and there became a familiar one. Soon it was common knowledge that the outcasts were being confined to the dungeons, where they were fed and sheltered, but not allowed to move freely outside their confines.

The castle became very clean and beautiful. No animal refuse to remove, no beggars to feed. And all of the remaining children were pleasing to the eye.

In their minds, the aristocracy was merely "cleaning up" so that their gentile eyes need never rest on anything that might upset them in any way.

They had no idea of the consequences of their actions.

♥The Children Are Taken Away

Serai noticed her friends beginning to disappear, one by one. She would come out to play in the morning, and find that her favorite horse, goat or coyote friend was nowhere to be found. Some had been put in stables or paddocks, and others were simply gone. Her heart grew heavy, and heavier still as she watched her little playmate with the twisted leg hobbling off in the charge of the castle guard.

She was beginning to understand what was happening, for Serai was wise beyond her years. And her sadness grew.

The formerly empty dungeons of Corazon were gradually becoming populated by some of Serai's most beloved companions. The only comfort she felt was in knowing that the children were protected and watched over by guardians, made up of the beasts and older outcasts who accompanied them there.

Although Serai loved the prosperous and self-righteous as much as anyone, she found that their judgment and fear prevented her from reaching them. She could no longer touch their hearts with her joy and radiant love as she had done in the past.

The nobility and upper classes slowly lost touch with the source of all that was truly good in their lives, as their focus became even stronger on the appearance of things.

As she watched the numbers of her friends gradually shrinking to only a few, Serai felt more and more alone. She could keep silent no longer.

"Mother, why are they taking so many below into the dungeons? I miss my friends!" Serai asked with some glimmer of hope that her mother might help.

But when she saw the look of resignation in her mother's eyes, her heart sank.

"It is the wish of Lord Peter, my dear. It is probably for the best. I don't fully understand it, but I must admit that things are much more tidy and clean now." Suddenly Serai felt a huge distance between herself and this woman she loved so much.

When Serai spoke again, it was in a small, quiet voice: "But they are my friends."

Her mother was silent.

And then, the inevitable happened.

♥ Serai Leaves Home

One night, while her parents were at the annual costume ball hosted by Lord Peter and Lady Delia, Serai packed a few of her favorite things in a burlap bag. Slinging the strap over her shoulder, the little girl looked carefully around her small room. She had a strange feeling she would never return. At ten years of age she really wasn't old enough to be making such a decision, yet it seemed there was no longer any choice.

Leaving a brief note for her parents, she pulled her cloak up to block the cold night air and set out in search of her beloved friends. As the heavy wooden door to her family's quarters closed behind her of its own accord, Serai sensed that nothing would ever be the same again.

For months before, Serai's parents Eva and Jorge had talked quietly in bed at night about the changes they saw in their precious daughter.

"You know what's happening to her friends, don't you Eva?" Jorge's voice was heavy in the darkness.

"Yes. And there's nothing we can do about it," came Eva's helpless reply.

On the night of her departure, thoughts of Serai were strong with her parents as they arrived home late from the palace ball, still dressed in their beautiful costume attire. Their expressions did not match the bright festive look of their clothing.

Just walking into their familiar quarters brought back the feeling of their daughter's sorrow.

The housemaid was asleep in the great room, as was usual when the couple was out late. A trusted servant for years, she had always watched well over their daughter's safety. Yet tonight, something felt wrong in the house.

Fighting a growing sense of panic, Jorge went straight to Serai's room.

A few moments later he returned, looking for Eva. "She's gone," were his only words to his wife when he found her undressing in their bedchambers. He handed Eva the note from Serai.

With trembling hands, the terrified woman read, "I've gone to be with my friends. Please don't worry about me. Love, Serai." Nothing more was written.

Frozen in her fear, Eva stared at the small slip of paper in her hands, hoping to somehow erase or make sense of what was happening.

The silence that filled the room between Eva and Jorge surprised them both. The warm glow from the wine at the ball was completely gone. They both knew what was happening, and had silently feared it for some time.

Jorge fought an almost uncontrollable urge to burst out his

front door in search of his daughter. Eva wanted to shout at him in anger because he wasn't already gone.

But their respect for their daughter's wishes and dignity was too great to forcibly require anything of her. She was not like other children. Though neither had ever said so, they actually felt inferior to her at times. The power she wielded in their hearts was extraordinary.

"I'll contact the guard at first light," Jorge said without looking at his wife. "There's no chance of finding her tonight."

As if both knew the thoughts of the other, they prepared for bed without speaking, knowing they would not sleep. Guilt and fear hung heavy on their hearts and in the air about them as they lay awake in silence.

As the first rays of sunlight reached out from the parapets across the inner castle walls, Jorge went in search of the castle guard. He felt like a coward for not conducting the search himself, but he was indeed afraid to face what he knew he would find.

When her husband returned an hour later, Eva was sitting at their kitchen table staring at a smoldering candlewick.

"I contracted with two castle guards to search for her," Jorge said. "They will contact us when they know something."

His words were too brief and the silence that followed too filled with their unspoken questions, fear and anger. They could already feel the distance between them growing.

After a long day of waiting for the knock at the door that would bring news of Serai, the couple sat down together to a lonely dinner, painfully aware of the empty place at the table. Neither spoke their daughter's name. The absence of her joyful, radiant spirit was a pain beyond what either could put into words.

Suddenly Jorge stirred as if jolted out of a trance. The sharp rapping at the outer door had to be one of the castle guards.

With a mix of eagerness and foreboding, Jorge rose quickly and went to the door, Eva's frozen eyes upon his back.

As Jorge ushered the tall, armored man into the entryway of their quarters, Eva joined them, standing behind her husband as if to shield herself from the pain she knew was coming.

The guard stood before them with his head down, a strange posture for this proud and powerful warrior. He did not relish this part of his job.

"She said to give you her love, m'lord and m'lady." He was silent for a moment. "She wishes not to hurt you, but she will not be returning to your home. She is determined to stay with her friends, though it's hard to believe anyone would choose to be in that dark and dreary place." The guard paused, shuffled his feet, and then continued hesitantly. "She is a special child, Your Worships. Her presence seems to bring much comfort to the ones confined to those miserable quarters. My comrade and I could not bring ourselves to return her to you forcibly."

"You were right in your decision." Eva was surprised to hear herself say in a hoarse whisper. "Thank you for your effort. We understand the will of our daughter and the special power she has. Go in peace." Handing the young man a single gold coin, Jorge ushered him out the door, raging silently at his own helplessness. As the guard stepped into the street, he turned suddenly and said, almost hopefully, "She said you could come to visit her any time."

But the door closed with no response.

♥Emerging Discontent

Lord Peter, Lady Delia and the "well to do" of Corazon had

no way of knowing what they had lost by relegating precious souls to the darkness. They slowly found themselves becoming more irritable with one another, less and less satisfied with their seemingly perfect lives.

There was more shouting and fighting in the taverns and in the marketplace than ever before, and occasional scuffles even erupted in the courtyards.

The lord and his lady began planning a long journey, purportedly for some high-level trade and negotiations. Secretly, however, they merely wished to be away from this castle that somehow no longer felt like a home.

The silence that followed Marguerite's words was full with sadness. It seemed to surround her listeners, gripping them in its hold. The old storyteller decided this was a fitting stopping point for now. "Let them live with these feelings for a while, and see what they learn of themselves," Marguerite thought to herself. The embers of the fire still pulsed against the darkness, fanned ever so lightly by the breeze. No one moved, as if hoping for some relief from their sorrow.

Finally the old woman stood slowly and looked up at the sky, saying to her group of listeners, "Come again when the moon's half full and we will continue our tale. Go now and take your rest, for tomorrow approaches with new stories of its own."

Six days hence, the afternoon was warm as the old storyteller slowly made her way up the long, winding stairs to the castle tower. The villagers had sent word that they would gather there to listen to more of her tale.

As the group arrived and settled into their customary circle, all eyes slowly moved to the wise old woman. The sound of her deep, resonant voice brought a hush over the gathering.

The sadness that entered the hearts of Corazon's inhabitants

started to feel normal. Like a silent invisible intruder, it had not announced its arrival. The comfort and joy they had once known was forgotten, as was its source.

Even Jorge and Eva managed to distract themselves with the busyness of everyday life, pushing their sorrow ever deeper. Amazingly, they never got around to going to the dungeons to visit their daughter Serai. Their fear of the darkness within them overcame their love, and their hearts slowly grew hard and cold like the walls of the castle.

♥ The Story of the Divine Child

Many years passed in the castle Corazon, and memories of the beasts and children took the form of a fable, a myth that told of a beautiful, divine child who had once lived among the commoners. It was said that she retreated into the shadows because of the confused will of the castle dwellers, and lived there in the darkness to this day. The story told of her joining the other children and condemned beasts in the lower realms, hiding with them there from harmful judgment.

According to the myth, the children never aged in the magical realms below, waiting quietly for that day when they might return to the open air and sunshine to roam and play freely once again.

The fable spoke also of the rejected adults, the poor and infirm that lived with the children and served as their protectors and guardians. And there were the exiled beasts, once free companions and now prisoners of the darkness, and the fiercest protectors of all.

Over time, these protectors became both guardian and jailer, serving to protect the children, yet keeping them captive at the same time.

The story of the divine child went on to tell of a few bright and brave souls who made journeys into the labyrinthine dungeons below the floors of Corazon, looking for the children in hopes of bringing them home. These were the rare ones who understood that the beasts and children were needed above, and belonged in the light of day. They knew that the hearts of the castle dwellers were empty and cold without the presence of the outcasts, and many problems existed because of their exile.

The journey into the dungeons below was difficult, however, and many sojourners did not return, or were changed forever by their experience. Survivors of the journey served to keep the myth alive, however, and to encourage others to make the journey who had the strength and the will to do so.

In spite of these efforts, the beasts and children remained below, and the fragmented life of those above continued.

Though many years passed, the story of the divine child never died. Some considered it worthless as a child's fairy tale, and others believed that it held truth and great meaning for their lives.

Chapter Two: Trouble in Aldea

His extraordinary skills in bargaining, trade and negotiation had made Marcelus the leading merchant in Corazon. This surprised no one, as his father had the same reputation for many years before him.

Their business was the trade of supplies and gold in the nearby village of Aldea and in the surrounding markets.

Marcelus commanded respect by his mere physical presence. Tall and striking, he attired himself impeccably to offset his dark wavy hair and ruddy complexion. His stature and quick manner gave the impression that he was always in charge. Only those paying very close attention noticed the occasional flash of insecurity in his hazel eyes, a feeling he covered with an air of poise and a habitually serious expression.

♥Marcelus' Story

Marcelus was born into a family where image and performance counted above all else. In fact, nothing else seemed to matter. Feelings and thoughts were only considered important if they led to looking good and succeeding.

His father Hector was a prime example of this approach to life. Though his pace of trading had slowed in recent years, the accomplished older merchant was a respected leader in both the community and the marketplace. His business acumen was still sharp and crisp when he chose to use it. At home as in business, Hector tolerated no laziness or what he called "worthless sentiment," and he made this very clear to his only son.

Marcelus found it impossible to meet his father's expectations, but that didn't stop him from trying. His father's love and approval meant everything to him. In his early efforts, he understandably fell short at just about everything he tried. Being of ill temper on a regular basis, Hector raged at his son, "No son of mine will be anything less than the best! Try again, and keep trying until no one can better you!"

When this happened, Marcelus just tried harder. Though he stumbled repeatedly in his efforts, he never gave up. The boy was determined to win his father's approval.

Over the years, many friends and family members remarked at the resemblance between Marcelus and Hector. "You're just like your father," they would say. "Work hard and one day you may be as good as he is!"

Marcelus always took these remarks as a challenge, and yet they were also a burden. He feared he would never emerge from his father's shadow, doomed to strive forever for an unreachable goal.

Sometimes, the strain of trying and never quite getting there was too much for Marcelus. Without wanting to, he would find himself succumbing to self-pity and despair as his father pushed him mercilessly.

"Why do I have to work all of the time? My friends are out hunting, exploring, and having fun. It seems like all I do is work!" the boy Marcelus once whined to his mother.

Entering the family chambers just in time to hear Marcelus' complaints, Hector flew into a rage, screaming, "What's wrong with you? Where is that sniveling going to get you? I'll have no son of mine whining and moping around. Never give up! I will make sure you keep going until you succeed! Now get out of my sight!"

Marcelus made the familiar journey to his room, followed soon and silently by his mother. This had happened far too many times...scolding and rejection from his father, followed by comfort and reassurance from his mother. This set up a pattern that would be with Marcelus for a long time.

The approval the boy secretly longed to receive from his father was never forthcoming. Hector could not give what he had never been given. He was passing on the family legacy that had been passed to him.

Never fulfilled or content, the two men lived lives of constant striving and silent desperation. No amount of actual success could ease their anxiety, or the tension between them.

Over the years, Marcelus found another kind of satisfaction that seemed to solve his problem. He developed a love of gold, the only substitute he could find for his father's love. Although his riches never filled the emptiness in his heart, he was nevertheless driven by his desire for more. And he became greatly skilled in the art of acquisition.

Marcelus secretly hoped that if he acquired enough gold, his father would one day give his blessing.

The towers of Corazon cast deep shadows that grew longer as the afternoon progressed. After a brief pause to pass around the wineskin filled with fresh spring water, Marguerite continued. As she began to speak, she leaned forward slightly to emphasize the drama of what she was about to tell.

♥ Trouble in the Village

After a particularly good run of luck in trading, Marcelus' fortune changed in one afternoon. His last two weeks of commerce in Aldea had been so lucrative that he was becoming a little over-confident in his abilities.

On a particularly quiet and ominously still evening, Marcelus made his way home from Aldea to Corazon. For a reason he could not explain, he felt distracted and anxious, despite his day of productive negotiating. The merchant tried to talk himself out of these feelings, to no avail.

Confused and frustrated, Marcelus hardly noticed that he had wandered down an unfamiliar roadway between market center and the village edge. So absorbed was he in his internal struggle that he ignored the instincts that bade him be wary as he ventured down the unfamiliar streets. Dusk threw shadows deep into the nooks and alleyways of the narrow, empty lane he had chosen.

Rounding a sharp corner, the merchant was suddenly alert. His eyes caught a movement to his left. Immediately his thoughts raced to the rumor of thieves and marauders lurking in this part of Aldea. Silently, he cursed himself for ignoring his instincts that would have taken him on a safer route. His body rigid now, the frightened merchant increased his pace.

They came from the shadows, five in number.

The silence with which the figures moved was eerie, otherwise. The dingily clad, disheveled men slowly moved in on the hapless merchant like wolves closing on their prey.

Marcelus felt a sudden tightness gripping his stomach like hot iron, as the silhouettes of his assailants became clearer. His body froze of its own accord and panic enveloped his mind as he realized what was about to happen.

In the far east parapet of Corazon, two of the castle guards leaned out over the walls and talked quietly. Both had noticed an uneasy feeling in the air. Sebastian, the older of the two, had long ago learned to trust his instincts and act on them. He was almost certain now that something had gone wrong in the village.

"Marcelus is usually back by this time of evening," he said to his comrade.

Turning abruptly away from his post, Sebastian gestured for the other guard to follow. "Gather eight warriors and join me at the castle gates. I fear the merchant may need us!"

Samantha carried out Sebastian's orders with the swiftness that only extensive training can bring. Though not as experienced as the senior guard, she too had sensed the merchant's need, and was eager to act on her instincts.

In only moments she alerted and was joined by several other dedicated castle guards, and in a swift flurry of coordinated action they joined Sebastian at the outer gates. With a nod from their leader, they burst through the castle gates and crossed the drawbridge, headed for Aldea.

"You'll pay dearly for your crimes," Marcelus growled at his assailants as he reluctantly handed over the last pouch of gold coins. One of the thieves held a dagger at his throat, and the merchant turned to stare at him in what was left of the fading light.

As Marcelus watched the shifting eyes of his assailant, the thief suddenly looked past him, and the merchant saw fear replace the fury in those eyes.

That's when Marcelus knew that help had arrived.

Shouts of anger filled the air as the warriors of Corazon burst upon the scene.

"Let none of them escape! They took it all!" Marcelus shouted as his attackers fell back into the shadows.

The flurry of swords, shields and clubs created a clatter and chaos that disoriented Marcelus, who was unused to combat. He quickly stepped aside to safety, trusting the trained castle guards to perform their duties without his involvement.

The fracas lasted only moments before the thieves realized they were outmatched. More vagabonds than fighters, they slunk away one by one, trailing blood into the darkness from whence they came.

"Let them go!" Sebastian commanded. "We will have ample opportunity to deal with them soon enough."

Then, turning to Marcelus, "M'lord, you're injured!"

Marcelus wiped what he thought was sweat from his eyes. It was only then that he saw the blood covering his hands and tunic. His face had been cut just below the hairline. The bewildered merchant had no idea how he had been wounded. Though the bleeding was profuse, his carefully exploring fingers told him it was only a shallow wound.

"It's just a scratch," he said while putting his scarf to his head to staunch the blood flow. "We have more important matters at hand. Was all of the gold recovered?" The merchant looked around at the castle guards inquisitively. One by one, they handed over the bags of coins they had recovered.

"Most of it is here," he said after a moment of counting. Looking up at his rescuers, the merchant added, "Well done!"

Breathing more easily now, the Corazon troupe looked around the area once more to make sure the thieves had indeed dispersed.

Marcelus remarked in a somber tone, "Well, we inflicted more harm than we took. I thank you for your help, Sebastian and all. I'd no doubt be lying here dead or dying had you not come when you did."

"Would we had arrived sooner, m'lord," spoke Sebastian as he surveyed the bloody brow of the merchant and the damage to some of his trusted comrades. "Those scoundrels would not have laid a finger on you, nor taken a single coin from your purse, had I been closer by!"

Marcelus smiled at Sebastian's devotion.

Weary, and grateful to be out of harm's way, the group made their way back to Corazon with the gold. All were in need of rest and healing.

Marguerite shifted uneasily as she prepared to enter the next part of the story. What she had to say now held great power, and she knew it would be disturbing to some. Giving particular focus to the younger and more volatile among her listeners, she began speaking once again.

Chapter Three: The Warrior Samantha

Another problem had arisen that day in the village, one that no one chose to discuss. In the midst of the fear and fury of battle, something had come over Samantha, the young female guard. Though accomplished for her age in the ways of combat, she was less experienced than the others.

For a few moments in the midst of the melee, it was as though she had become someone else. As Samantha and her comrades waded into the fray, she pivoted, swirled and swung her sword at one after another of her adversaries. Her golden hair streaming like flames from beneath her helmet, the fiery warrior exuded intense passion. Never had she felt more alive. The urge to victory filled her body with the desire to destroy, and the combination was explosive.

One moment from that day stood frozen in her mind for years to follow.

♥ Blood Lust in Battle

Amid the dust, sweat, curses and cries of pain, Samantha raised her sword over the exposed torso of a fallen assailant. Her muscles pulsing with power, the young combatant felt an exhilarating surge running through her body. It seemed for an instant that she wanted nothing more than to kill her helpless foe. The smell of blood and the adrenaline coursing through her veins had taken her over the edge of sensibility. In the chaos of the moment, she felt something wild erupting within her.

That something wanted to kill.

At the moment Samantha raised her sword for the fatal blow to her disarmed opponent, Sebastian happened to see her. In an instant, he took in the entire scene and knew what was happening. An experienced warrior, he had seen this before.

His powerful voice leapt from his chest, "Samantha!"

The young woman's sword froze in midair, and a flood of awareness returned to her. As if waking from a dream, she was suddenly shocked at what she was about to do. Lowering her sword, she kicked the frightened man away from her and watched him as he scrambled back into the shadows.

Afterward, no one talked about this particular event, though most of those present had seen what happened.

Fighting—and even killing—for protection and self-preservation was one thing, but killing a defenseless opponent was something else entirely. When Sebastian so urgently called Samantha's name, those who heard his voice instinctively knew what had happened.

The other warriors had no words of counsel for her, for they knew and feared the same forces in themselves.

Coming to love violence was an occupational hazard in their profession as warriors. They knew all too well what it could do, and how it could slowly drive a person insane, causing them to kill senselessly, for killing's sake.

No warrior wanted to suffer the fate of becoming one who loved—and lived—to kill.

Samantha had actually enjoyed the feeling of blood lust that consumed her during that moment in Aldea. The brief moment of violent passion had given her a taste of a power she had known only once before, during an incident in her warrior training.

And now Samantha had crossed a threshold, and had no idea how to go back. Her shameful secret was that the dark force within her actually felt good—at the same time that it horrified her. The warrior found herself in a deep inner turmoil of fear and fascination.

The tension eased in Marguerite's face as she moved out of this part of the story. She paused, breathing deeply. As her listeners sensed her shift, they too relaxed and breathed more easily. When she continued, it was in a softer tone.

"I am growing tired of these daily journeys into the marketplace," Marcelus confided to Samantha. They were sipping mead near the western parapet of the castle overlooking the forest, as the golden colors of day's end spread across the horizon. "Ever since those thieves attacked me, I have lost my desire to work. I know that many here in Corazon depend on me. I just can't get my old enthusiasm back."

Samantha only listened. She understood, yet she had no answers for the merchant. Having met for the first time following the village brawl, the two were just getting acquainted. She was not ready to tell him of her own inner struggles.

♥ Strange Sounds

"Sometimes at night I am disturbed by strange noises," Marcelus confided after a moment had passed.

Samantha felt a sudden tightness in her stomach at Marcelus' words.

"There seems to be some kind of crying and moaning sound coming from the lower regions of the castle. I feel an urge to go and see what it is, and yet I don't go."

Again Samantha said nothing. She, too, had heard the sounds, deep in the night when she was alone in her bedchambers. A chill ran up her spine as she recalled the eerie sensation of the screeching sound that seemed to come from within and all around her at the same time. After the two sat for another awkward moment of silence, she excused herself with the pretense of needing some rest.

"I need to work early tomorrow." She paused again, then, "I'll bid you goodnight now, Marcelus."

Over the next few days, Samantha discovered through casual conversation that the other warriors had heard the strange sounds also. Not wanting to appear shaken or afraid, the guards of Corazon spoke in casual tones, their manner indicating that this was of no great concern to them. "It's only the wind whistling through the towers," Sebastian stated with an effort at showing complete confidence. "Pay it no mind. We have more important things to worry over."

But Sebastian knew there was something extraordinary and somehow significant about these sounds. He grew steadily more concerned as he watched the change that came over his friends and charges. They grew edgy and ill tempered from lack of sleep. They were quick to anger. Fights and loud disputes erupted far too often. This was disturbing to the merchants and other citizens of Corazon. They never knew when there would be another fight or argument in the courtyard, or in the warrior's quarters or training arena. The comfort and security of Corazon was being diminished daily.

"Something must be done, Marcelus!" Samantha insisted, hoping that the merchant could use his influence to bring about needed change. She had come to visit the merchant in his chambers, and the two were sharing fresh fruit and wine. She leaned toward her handsome friend and put her hand on his forearm to show the depth of her concern. "It is getting worse by the day. I've never seen the warriors like this. For the first time, I find myself questioning their bravery. It is even starting to affect Sebastian, and I never thought anything could ruffle him!"

The merchant did not move. He put his half-raised goblet back on the stone table without taking a drink. Transfixed, he stared into the smoldering embers of his evening fire. Then as if waking from a dream, he turned and looked at Samantha.

Marcelus was instantly and incongruously aware of her striking beauty, her golden hair framing the strong features of her bronzed face in the firelight. It was as if he were seeing her for the first time. Her womanhood overshadowed the familiarity of friendship, and for a brief moment he imagined being with her in an intimate way. In that moment he remembered nothing she had said.

Suddenly, both were embarrassed.

"Perhaps we should consult the wizard Magus," Samantha said distractedly, not wanting to acknowledge the look she had caught in Marcelus' eye. "He may possibly be willing to help us."

Angry for no good reason, Marcelus blurted out, "No!"

Grateful to be rescued from his vulnerable longing, the

merchant allowed himself to be swept into the old, familiar feelings of anger and rebellion.

Out from under his father's controlling influence, it was difficult for Marcelus to ask for help of any kind. Samantha's suggestion to consult Magus had triggered this very resistance. A little surprised at the intensity of her friend's reaction, Samantha waited.

Then, in a slightly milder tone the merchant said, "We must resolve this on our own. Let's meet and speak of it again on Thursday next, and see if our musings have brought new wisdom."

Right now Marcelus just wanted to be away from Samantha, with the futile hope that she hadn't noticed the hunger in his eyes.

Wondering over what had just occurred, Samantha agreed to meet and discuss the topic again. The two parted company without their usual warmth, and felt strangely alone as they went their separate ways.

Marguerite checked for signs of fatigue as the water skin was passed once again. Yes, this was enough for now. The eyes of her listeners told her that they needed time to be with the pieces of the story that she had given them so far. "Go and think on these things," she said softly. "We will gather again on the morrow, when you've taken your rest."

Chapter Four: Into the Depths

The faithful gathering reconvened under the spreading oak in the castle courtyard, ready and waiting for the continuing story. Only one among them seemed distracted. A little boy squirmed and whimpered in his mother's arms. Marguerite smiled softly at the boy and his mother. She planned to begin the storytelling when the wineskin had made its rounds.

While gathering her thoughts for the next telling, Marguerite found her attention drawn once again to the agitated child in his mother's arms. The boy was wriggling in earnest now, and starting to cry. The young woman looked around in embarrassment, and rose to leave.

"Give him to me." The crone's imposing voice stopped the young mother in her tracks. She was surprised to feel the older woman's vigorous attention focused on her. "Your son and those like him play a significant role in our story. We must embrace our troubled children, and keep them with us. I'll tend him a while, so you both may stay with us." In the arms of Marguerite, the boy's agitation seemed to melt. He gazed into the crone's deep, dark eyes as if in a trance, and became very still.

Then, raising her magical eyes to the waiting crowd of listeners, Marguerite resumed her tale of the mysteries unfolding in the castle Corazon. The vibrant resonance of the crone's voice soon lulled the boy into a deep sleep.

The chilling cries from beneath Marcelus' chambers were bothering him more with every passing day. Many nights, he lay awake staring into the darkness, unable to tell if the sounds were inside or outside his head.

There it was again. It sounded like a child crying out in pain and torment, or a beast howling in its misery.

The resulting lack of sleep began to tell on the merchant's work. His actions were fraught with increasing struggle and difficulty. He knew he could not go on like this much longer.

The awkwardness he felt with Samantha was no help. Marcelus no longer felt as comfortable with her since his amorous feelings had emerged. All of this left him with a feeling of emptiness in his heart.

Desperate to ease his anxiety, Marcelus decided to make a journey into the labyrinth beneath the castle on his own. He was almost certain now that the cries came from there.

Yet the merchant's reluctance to go to the lower realms was huge. Stories of hideous beasts hiding in twisted tunnels and dark caverns had scared him since he was a child. And now he was considering going there alone.

As the time of departure approached, his fear did not subside. Nor did his resolve.

In the late hours of a dark, stormy night, the merchant left his chambers quietly. He wanted no one to know of his expedition.

Using the hood of his cloak to shield against the rain, Marcelus ventured into the open courtyard and down a roadway that led to the labyrinth entrance.

Moving from the road down a narrow rain-drenched walkway, he shuddered as much from inner as outer chill. Finding the dungeons within the labyrinth could prove a difficult task in and of itself. The unwary could easily get lost in the confusing network of passageways.

These thoughts and fears were strong in the merchant as he stood before the vine-covered doorway leading to the labyrinth stairway. Hidden away in a dark corner of a small and little used plaza, it had a foreboding look and feel about it. Most of the quarters in this area of the castle were empty and cluttered, as if no one wanted to live near the portal to the dark realms.

As Marcelus stood there frozen in a quandary, his mind reviewed a lifetime of memories, myths and fables that had been imparted to him one way or another. He had heard that there were elders who made regular descents to these lower regions, an interest he had never understood until now.

And there was the story of the divine child told to him as a boy, which hinted that these journeys might bring valuable healing and self-discovery.

Yet these thoughts brought the merchant no comfort. What frightened him most as he stood in the cold rain staring at the foreboding doorway were the stories about those who had never returned from their subterranean sojourns.

Realizing that he had stopped breathing during these racing thoughts, the merchant stepped back a few steps, took a few deep breaths, and approached again.

♥ The Journey Begins

Time seemed to slow as the merchant reached for the massive iron ring in the middle of the oaken door before him. As it slowly creaked open, the darkness on the other side seemed to reach out blindly in his direction.

Looking over his shoulder as he stepped inside, Marcelus surveyed the plaza cautiously. He did not want to be seen by anyone, lest he might have to explain himself. He pulled the heavy door shut behind him.

Inside, the darkness closed in on the merchant as if eager to have him in its grasp. A wave of nausea passed through his midsection, followed by a mild sensation of dizziness in his head.

A peal of thunder from outside the doorway seemed muffled and far away.

With trembling hands, Marcelus lit his lantern.

With resolve as frail as the lantern light penetrating the darkness before him, the merchant slowly took his first steps across the landing toward the descending stairway.

Making his way carefully down the winding flight of stone steps, Marcelus thought briefly of Samantha and her suggestion that they consult the wizard for guidance. Magus knew these realms well, and would no doubt have been of great assistance.

But he was already here, and alone.

As Marcelus arrived at the bottom of the staircase, he was dismayed to find yet another set of stairs descending off to his left.

His mind raced with thoughts like, "This part of the castle is an entire world unto itself. Anything could happen here, and no one would ever know the truth of it." Yet the merchant continued to push onward.

Compelled forward by a will that no longer seemed his own, the wary merchant used his free hand to feel his way along the damp stone walls of the cramped, narrow descent.

The silence in this place was so complete that the sound of his breathing and footfall seemed deafening. At the bottom of the second stairwell, he stopped to rest and reorient himself.

Just as the merchant was catching his breath and beginning to feel a little calmer, a strange, alien sound began slowly and then grew within his field of awareness. Soon the noise was so formidable that it seemed to come from all around him, with shape and color of its own.

Riveted by the noise, Marcelus' mind raced among possible explanations of its origin.

With the weight of unpleasant familiarity, it steadily dawned on him that this was that same chilling sound that he had been hearing in his chambers at night. Only now it was much closer, louder, and more real.

As frightened as he was, he remembered that this was exactly the reason he had come to the labyrinth...to discover the origin of that sound.

Yet knowing that he was drawing closer to his goal of solving the mystery gave the merchant no relief.

And the wailing continued, growing even louder now.

Marcelus could feel the sound in his gut, pulling and tearing at his insides as if it were alive within him.

Pushing hard against his own fear and a growing desire to retreat, he continued.

Three dark openings departed from the landing where the merchant now stood. He was somehow drawn to the one directly in front of him.

His lantern seemed to be losing its battle with the darkness. The stale, musty air moved thick and heavy around him, pressing in from all directions. Shadows in the cracks and crevices shivered and shook in response to the flickering light, creating the illusion of movement all around.

Things were getting no better as Marcelus progressed on his journey. The sound was growing louder and more chaotic now, and with it the pain in his stomach became unbearable.

Then all progress stopped.

Stark terror took the merchant in its icy grasp. He was totally paralyzed by fear. Try as he may, he could not move nor cry out.

And at that moment the sound changed.

A low, menacing growl slowly emerged from below the wailing, growing until it had replaced the higher sound with a primitive, guttural snarl.

Marcelus' muscles jumped and twitched under his cold, clammy skin. All he wanted now was to be free of this place, to return to the comfortable familiarity of his everyday life.

♥The Beast

A quick movement caught Marcelus' eye just outside the ring of light cast by his lantern. As his eyes adjusted, the image of a half-human beast with piercing red eyes began to clarify. Sharp, uneven fangs filled a hideous, gaping hole that was its mouth. Crouched on all fours and covered with splotches of hair occasionally revealing hideously pink skin, it was poised and ready to strike. But it did not.

The growling had stopped. Now the sound came from Marcelus.

He could not stop the sound that erupted from his throat as he saw the creature leap toward his throat. His own terrified scream and the attack of the beast merged in one explosive instant, and passed.

The fallen lantern still flickered on the stone floor, and there was no beast.

Marcelus scanned his body for injuries, and found none. Shaking his head to regain his senses, he realized he could move freely again.

In an uncoordinated flurry of action, the merchant grabbed his lantern and scrambled wildly toward the staircase, daylight and sanity. Looking frequently over his shoulder, he stumbled and fell every few steps.

Nothing followed.

Without really knowing how he had found his way back, the distraught merchant burst through the oaken door and collapsed onto the courtyard gasping for air.

No daylight greeted him. The rain had stopped, and stars flickered brightly overhead.

As his familiar sense of reality returned, Marcelus looked around. He was embarrassed by his fear and erratic behavior, glad that no one was there.

The absurdity of his situation both sobered and worried

the merchant as he made his way back to his chambers. His thoughts raced as he tried to make sense of what had happened, to reassure himself that he was not insane.

"Could I have made this all up?" He answered his own question in his mind, "No! I know what I heard and I know what I saw."

The merchant's frustration built and grew stronger until...a shift occurred. He was suddenly angry at his own helplessness. "I won't let this get the better of me. I'll figure it out whatever it takes!"

His fear became a fierce determination to solve the mystery. This new feeling of focus calmed him, and he was almost back to his usual level of confidence by the time he reached his chambers.

In the familiar comfort of his bed, the experience in the labyrinth seemed like a distant dream. And yet sleep eluded him for a while.

Lying in the stillness of early morning and watching the new day's light chase the shadows across his bed, Marcelus was surprised and relieved at the fading of his fears.

As consciousness slowly faded from his mind, however, a dream image drifted briefly before him. A small boy was huddled alone in gray shrouds, quiet in a small dark chamber. At the entrance to the boy's quarters, a hideous hair-covered, half-human beast with red eyes stood vigilant watch.

The little boy in Marguerite's arms was sleeping quietly as the story came to a pause. The crone returned the sleeping child to his mother, as the evening's remaining light faded softly behind the courtyard walls.

"The little ones are our guides and teachers," she said softly, as if to herself. "We must always honor the emotions and the needs of our children, for they point us to the lost and forgotten parts of ourselves." Pausing a moment, she added in a slightly louder voice, "For our next meeting, we will find a place on a hilltop north of Corazon. It will serve us well to have a good view of the castle walls as we continue our story."

After sending her listeners on their way, Marguerite stood watching as the last few disappeared under the archway. She smiled, musing softly to herself. "We are all children, but we have forgotten." With this the wise old woman turned toward the last light of the departing day, giving thanks for its blessings.

Chapter Five: The Sword and Shield

It was a full fortnight before the group gathered again. Summer's solstice celebrations had taken everyone's time and focus, and the activities of daily life were a constant distraction. Several of her listeners had come to Marguerite in the interim, however, to ask when their next session would be. The skillful raconteur had created a hunger in their hearts, and she knew she must not wait too long before the next telling.

After breaking their fast together in the castle gardens one bright Sunday morning, Marguerite and her little party gathered up the bundles of supplies they had for the day's outing. They had each packed food and drink as instructed by the crone, to keep them comfortable throughout the day. With the tall, gaunt storyteller as their guide, the small troupe made their way into the green rolling hills that surrounded Corazon. After an hour's walk, they settled on the crest of the highest knob overlooking their castle home.

When stillness gathered among her listeners, the crone resumed her tale. Standing now, Marguerite felt her body filling with the warm, familiar power of her tale.

♥ Samantha's Story

In the years before Samantha wielded her sword in battle in Aldea, her life journey had taken her along a challenging road.

She had distinguished herself in her family as a very sensitive child. While this was written off to her gender, it was far more than just a contrast to her three brothers. Samantha was somehow able to feel the pain of the people around her, which was both her blessing and her curse. It was a blessing as it bore testimony to her open heart, and a curse because no one recognized that it was a blessing.

Her sensitivity shifted the unclaimed emotional burden of her family to her shoulders. It seemed somehow that it was her job to bear their pain.

Though tears may have been tolerated at times, Samantha was not allowed to show anger. The sharp blade of her anger rarely left its hiding place throughout her childhood. But a bright flame burned within her, showing up in her dreams and working in her mind to form the views she held of herself and the world.

Warrior dreams sprang early to the energetic mind of this precocious girl-child. The bright rapier of her wit and will formed itself in her imagination such that she knew that one day she would wield a sword of her own.

Her family's home was an oak cabin, on the edge of the great forest north of Corazon. Her father, a stout quiet man, was a woodsman and traditional in his ways. He held no store for a woman or girl being out of her place. Samantha learned early she was to stay beside her mother and learn a woman's ways.

Samantha's brothers, on the other hand, accompanied their father to the forest and learned the family trade of woodcutting, as had been their tradition for generations.

None of this set well with Samantha. She could not bear staying cooped up while her brothers went off to the woods with their father. Yet that is what happened, day after day. It seemed at times she would erupt with the envy and resentment she held inside.

Beneath these feelings, however, a deeper passion was brewing. Though she had spoken of it to no one, Samantha knew a secret.

Her room shared a wall with her parents' bedroom, thus only she heard the hushed late night conversations that would serve to change her life forever.

Lying quietly in her bed in the darkness, the child Samantha could hear her father's muffled voice well enough to make out his words, "You have no right to object to my wishes, woman. Just do your job and stay out of my way. You're to come when I need you and be quiet when I don't. That daughter of yours is the same as you are...neither of you content with what I have provided. Always wanting something more, something not rightfully yours. Shut up your complaining now and go to sleep."

Sometimes it got much worse than that. Her father's voice would get louder, and occasionally there were sounds of physical struggle. Once Samantha heard a thud, and imagined her mother falling to the floor...but she could not be sure.

Samantha never heard her mother's voice in these late night encounters. Its soft resonance could not penetrate even the interior walls. It was only the timbre of her father's barrel-chested rumble that carried his words to her innocent ears.

Unable to sleep on the nights of her parents' quarrels, Samantha vowed to herself again and again that she would stand up to her father one day. She felt it was her job to defend not only herself but her mother as well. She prayed for the strength to protect her mother from the oppression of her father's persecution. The opportunity never came.

The day after Samantha's fourteenth birthday, her father dropped dead in the forest. He was pushing himself too hard, as he had so many times before. This time, however, his heart refused to cooperate, and without warning struck its last beat as his ax hovered midair over a felled oak.

A half hour later her brothers stood in the cabin doorway like mournful statues, silhouetted to their mother by the evening sun behind them. No sooner were their mumbled words spoken than the stricken woman collapsed sobbing to the floor. Samantha knelt by her side, feeling numb and cold.

In a state of shock from her loss, Samantha was surprised at the sudden turn of her thoughts. With deep regret and despair, she realized that now she could never fully prove herself to him. She could never show him that he was wrong about her. And she could never win his love.

Samantha's path had long been set, and her father's death only strengthened her convictions. She kept him alive in her heart and mind, and with a quiet resolve went about the business of proving herself to him, as if he were watching.

The family was completely different now. Samantha's mother no longer felt safe in the cabin without her husband, despite the strength and reassurance of her sons.

Much to the dismay of the boys, Samantha's mother soon was making preparations to move. She had found a new dwelling inside the walls of the castle Corazon. Finding it necessary to work to support her family, she sought employment as a kitchen maid, and did not hesitate when the job was offered her. Two of her sons stayed behind to continue the woodcutting business, and the third came along to find work in the castle.

Removed from the tyranny of her father and a life not of her choosing, Samantha thrived in the castle life with its options and opportunities. As a result of her soul-felt determination to prove herself to all men, she developed an unusual level of power and aggression. Her body began to form itself according to the vision of what she chose to become, and soon she looked every bit the warrior of her dreams.

Long, wavy blond hair hung loose around the blossoming young woman's shoulders. Though of average height, her stance and posture gave the impression that she was large and powerful. The proportions of her body were somewhat masculine in dimension, though not at the expense of a very appealing essence of feminine beauty.

Samantha's most striking feature was her eyes. No one attempting to describe the girl's eyes failed to use the word "piercing".

♥ Sebastian's Shield

One morning while performing routine errands around her castle quarters, Samantha had a most unusual encounter.

As the stout Sebastian rounded the corner just ahead of her, sunlight flashed through the parapet of the east tower and caught the shiny surface of his shield. Blinded briefly by the flash of light, Samantha shielded her eyes from its brilliance.

Seeing what had happened, Sebastian lowered his shield.

Samantha looked up as her vision slowly adjusted, and her eyes found his. Her breath caught briefly in her throat. She was struck as much by his expression of gentle strength in his dark brown eyes as she had been by the gleaming light from his shield.

"I did not mean to startle you," Sebastian stated in a formal tone, making every effort to conceal his immediate attraction to the beautiful young woman before him. "I've just polished my shield, and the sun must have hit it just right to reflect in your eyes. Please accept my humblest apologies." The man's manner touched a place in Samantha's heart, and she secretly hoped that they would become friends. She quickly surveyed his beautiful ebony skin tone and muscular physique, trying not to be obvious in her interest. Then, feeling shy about her thoughts, she commented on his shield.

"That is the most beautiful shield I have ever seen!" Samantha exclaimed. "Who crafted it for you?"

Embarrassed at her praise, Sebastian looked down at the heavy work of wood, leather and polished metal on his arm. He then replied quietly, "I made it myself," and looking up continued with, "My name is Sebastian." He offered his hand in greeting to the young woman. "My family and I are builders of shields and structures."

As they talked, Samantha found herself fascinated by this man and his craft. It occurred to her that she had never met anyone quite so self-contained and mild in temperament.

Sebastian explained to her that his family's work had been to provide strength and protection for the castle dwellers for many generations. He mentioned with some pride that his ancestors had designed and built the great walls that surrounded the castle itself.

Pausing for a moment, Marguerite guided her listeners' gaze toward the walls surrounding Corazon, which looked somehow more impressive from their hilltop view. After only a brief moment, she continued.

"And where did you receive your warrior training?" Samantha asked Sebastian, surprised at her own boldness.

"I was apprenticed to the shield master at the warrior training camp just beyond the hills there." Though comforted by listening to Sebastian describe his craft, Samantha became unexplainably distracted the moment she heard the words, "warrior training camp." Her deep restlessness grew until it was unrelenting. Unable to maintain the composure needed for polite conversation, she made an excuse about needing to be elsewhere, and took her leave in an awkward manner.

As Sebastian watched her walk away and disappear around the corner, he wondered if he had somehow offended her. Hoping they would meet again, the young shield maker returned to his duties with a grudging sadness that was unfamiliar to him. In the ensuing days, Sebastian thought often of Samantha, and of her beauty and intensity. Despite his attraction, he somehow knew he was destined to be with her only as a companion and friend.

♥ Samantha Leaves Corazon

Something deep and powerful inside Samantha wanted release. It became increasingly clear to her that she could not stay with her mother in the mundane life she had created. The plan brewing in her mind for weeks slowly came to fruition a few days after her meeting with Sebastian.

On a cool, breezy afternoon in early spring, Samantha decided to leave Corazon to seek apprenticeship at the warrior training camp. The desire was awakened the moment Sebastian mentioned it to her.

Though historically warrior training was reserved for males, it was rumored that girls were now being accepted, as long as they were able to endure the rigors of the training.

Samantha was determined to qualify, no matter what it took. Somehow it seemed that her very life depended on it.

More than anything, she was determined to seek advanced instruction in the use of the sword. She felt that somehow its mastery would enable her to cut through the bonds and restrictions that she had felt around her since birth.

In the quiet of that very night, as her family slept, the passionate young woman prepared for her journey. Gathering a few provisions, she bound her hair and tucked it under her hat. Appearing as a man would allow her to pass more freely throughout the castle.

Her mother and brothers would never approve of what she was doing. And her father, were he alive, would have furiously forbade it. Her family's unwillingness to recognize her true nature created a feeling of absolute necessity that she break free or perish.

Even with the fierceness of her determination, sadness lingered about Samantha's heart as she slung her knapsack over her shoulder and stepped out into the darkness. Looking back at her family's quarters, she spoke a silent goodbye to the life she had known. Turning away into the night, she steeled herself against her sorrow and the bite of cold night air.

Marguerite stretched and yawned. This was a good place for a pause in the story. When she announced the break, the little group slowly dispersed, some stretching out on the grass and others strolling off alone or in pairs into the forest.

After an hour or so, naps, nourishment and walks were taken and the members of the small party reappeared to take their places. The old storyteller settled back into her tale. Someone had built a fire during the interlude, to prepare for the cooler evening hours ahead.

Chapter Six: The Calling From Below

Following his aborted journey to the unknown regions of Corazon, Marcelus was more bothered than ever by the wailing and howling from the dungeons. Having come closer to the pain of those locked away there, he found that he was more sensitive to pain of all kinds. When he heard the cries of children, it was as if he felt their pain in his own heart.

Life on the surface of things continued, of course. He maintained his daily sojourns into Aldea to peddle his wares, in spite of his loss of sleep and growing irritability.

But his heart was not in his work any more.

It was a warm summer afternoon, and Marcelus was closing down the wagon from which he customarily displayed his goods for sale. Suddenly his attention was drawn to a large, powerful looking man striding rapidly past him. With a start, the merchant became aware that the man was holding one of the little village waifs by the arm, literally dragging the child bodily across the cobblestones.

Marcelus knew this particular boy from previous encounters in the village, and had felt an unexplained kinship with him. There was something about the constant look of sorrow in the lad's big eyes that always seemed to stir the merchant's emotions. He was surprised the lad had not been taken away to the dungeons like others of his kind, and secretly hoped the boy could escape that fate.

And here he was again, dressed in his usual rags and making grunting sounds of frustration and anger as he struggled in vain to break free from the big man's iron grip.

Marcelus was surprised to discover a white-hot rage leaping up from inside him. When he saw the red marks on the boy's arm and the blood trickling from the corner of his mouth, the merchant could be still no longer.

Without really knowing what he was doing and with no clear plan in mind, Marcelus flashed across the distance that separated him from the passing man. As if something inside him knew what to do, he deftly wrenched the muscular arm of the man so that the boy was instantly free. Shocked by the unexpected interruption, the stranger stood aghast. For a few brief seconds, both men watched as the terrified urchin scampered away as fast as his skinny little legs could manage.

Still surging with the power of his rage, Marcelus turned to look up into the big man's eyes, which burned now with a fire of their own. The two stood there for what seemed like an eternity, the wild gaze of each locked on the other. At last, just when Marcelus was certain that he was about to be pummeled severely, the stranger wheeled around and stormed off down the street without a word.

Surprised at his good fortune, Marcelus noticed with some relief that the man was not even pursuing the boy.

Pushing his wagon back to the castle later that night, Marcelus reviewed these events in his mind.

It occurred to him that his action on behalf of the boy had been entirely impulsive. It was as if something inside him had taken over against his will. He wanted to believe that the man worked for Lord Peter or the magistrate, and was hauling the urchin off to the dungeons. That would have somehow justified his actions. But in his calmer mood now, he just wasn't sure.

For all he knew, the lad may have been beaten by other boys, or injured in some type of accident and the man may in fact have been a rescuer. The boy's resistance may have only been a reflection of his fear and confusion.

The stranger may have been trying to help, and now Marcelus would never know the truth of it.

It gradually dawned on the merchant that his actions had more to do with his frayed emotions than the reality of the boy's situation. He had projected his own fear and pain onto this hapless child, and the ensuing rage blinded him.

Walking through the large open gates of Corazon, Marcelus encountered the familiar sights, sounds and smells of his home. He thought again of his trip to the dungeons. He was starting to realize that his mind was clouded when he faced the pain of others. His inner turmoil created a haze in his vision that prevented clarity and focus. This awareness sobered the young merchant, and he silently vowed to tell no one of the day's events.

The cold in the air grew sharp now, as the moonless night descended upon the little group of listeners. Silently lighting her torch from the remaining embers in the fire, Marguerite prepared to lead her weary troupe back to the castle. The wise old storyteller was hoping that the silence of the night would cause them to hold the story's images in their imaginations a little longer.

"Such mysteries deserve time and space of their own, and need not be too soon mixed with casual chatter and drivel." Standing, the crone spoke these words almost absently into the fire, and yet everyone present knew her message was for them. Slowly, she turned and led the way back to the castle, her torch flickering and casting long shadows along the darkened path.

♥ Samantha's Inner Battle

Marguerite chose the village square in Aldea as the setting for the next segment of her saga. She and her following were to meet under the old oak tree near the fountain, where they would be undisturbed by the passing pedestrians.

The crone was the first to arrive, and she quietly made her place near the base of the oak. Sunlight filtered softly through the leaves overhead while the listeners trickled in and formed their circle.

As a quiet sense of anticipation slowly arose within her murmuring audience, the wise woman began to speak. Her resonant voice easily acquired the full attention of her listeners.

Samantha felt the fire of familiar rage welling up inside her as her practice opponent carelessly dropped his shield. He seemed to think he could easily take her without even defending himself, simply because she was a girl. In a movement too quick for his eye to follow, the point of her sword was at the throat of the surprised young man.

In a sudden burst of fury that surprised even her, Samantha was wishing for true battle—not merely training. The urge to kill this obnoxious, over-inflated swordsman was almost

overwhelming to her. His attitude of confident bravado reminded her all too much of her father. If not for the quiet voice in the back of her mind, she would indeed have destroyed him. The muscles in her arm and shoulder rippled beneath taut skin as she struggled to restrain the killer instinct that surged within her. The wild and unfamiliar presence possessed her almost fully. As if it had a mind of its own, she felt its longing to see the point of her sword plunge into the soft flesh and release the arrogant opponent's life-blood onto the ground.

Slowly the blood lust passed. Samantha took a breath and relaxed her muscles ever so slightly. As her normal consciousness returned, she decided to merely frighten the man and teach him a lesson in humility and respect.

Shock and embarrassed rage flooded the young man's face as he struggled in vain to maneuver free. But every slight movement only served to bring the tip of Samantha's sword further into the already stretched skin of his neck. Something in his eyes seemed to die or depart, as he realized this woman had bested him.

Many of the men in the camp disliked the idea of females being part of the warrior training, and defeat by one of them in combat was almost more than this young warrior could stomach. His companions watched as his frustration built near to exploding, and then they watched him sink into helplessness and surrender.

Slowly, and with the slightest hint of a smile, Samantha lowered and sheathed her sword. Then she walked casually back to her designated place on the training ground, as if nothing important had happened. Silence reigned among the watchers. Her defeated, humiliated opponent raised himself slowly and joined his comrades, his eyes lowered to the ground.

In spite of a few such moments of triumph, Samantha found the warrior training to be extremely demanding. At times the discipline required of her seemed too much. Her restless spirit yearned to be free from the schedules of rigorous exercise and practice.

Samantha often feared that she would be dismissed from training. Her quick temper combined with the fact of her being female made her feel vulnerable to more than the usual scrutiny.

Her few shortcomings were overlooked by the well-seasoned Master Warriors, however. Her unflagging determination and passionate manner far outweighed any limitations she may have had. A few months into the training, she had won her teachers' respect.

The training lasted over two years, with few breaks other than summer holiday to visit home and family. It was acceptable, however, for second year warriors-in-training to seek employment as castle guards during their break. It was on one such interlude that Samantha had met Marcelus and struck up what proved to be an enduring friendship. It was also during that same time that the two had their encounter with the thieves in Aldea.

And now her training was complete. She had been honored as a full-fledged warrior with all privileges, having completed even the most difficult of the challenges laid before her.

Greater than her joy over having completed her tasks, however, was Samantha's relief at the thought of a break from the swords, shields and sweat. She found herself looking forward to seeing her family and her friends Sebastian and Marcelus, back at home in the castle Corazon.

♥ Return to the Inner Journey

The merchant and Samantha developed a powerful bond, the day she and the other guards had come to his rescue in the village brawl. Sharing the intensity of that ominous moment had connected them to each other in an unusual way. Different as they were, both found a comfort in the other's presence. There seemed a kind of destiny in their unexplained alliance.

For his part, Marcelus had much to tell Samantha on her return from her warrior training. He spoke with a quiet sense of urgency about the night callings and his aborted attempt to find their source.

"As awful as it was, I simply must return, Samantha. I am now planning another journey into the labyrinth. Will you join me?" Marcelus extended the invitation with a sideways glance at his friend, a little ashamed that he did not feel confident returning alone. They were standing near the main courtyard of Corazon, where they had met shortly after Samantha's arrival from the training camp.

Samantha found the prospect intriguing, and she admired the merchant's courage. Though he seemed unaware of it himself, she sensed a deep power within the handsome Marcelus, and it was strongly reflected in his desire to explore the depths.

Something about traversing unknown magical realms below the courtyards of Corazon appealed to Samantha. She accepted Marcelus' invitation, and they began discussing their plans while strolling casually through the castle gardens. The mix of fear and excitement was still high when they said goodbye and made their separate ways to their quarters.

As the agreed upon date for their journey drew closer, the two companions became more and more anxious about their decision. Marcelus was not sleeping well, and Samantha was having recurring nightmares in which she was lost in a labyrinth, unable to find her way out.

Several days after their initial meeting, the two were together for a lunch of roast goat and mead in a small tavern near the merchant's quarters.

"There are powerful forces at work in the dungeons, and I understand little of how to deal with them. I am compelled to go, and yet I feel ill prepared." This time Marcelus did not look at Samantha as he spoke, attempting to draw on an inner strength to face his limitations.

Samantha remained silent. She was thinking of Magus, but chose not to bring him up to Marcelus again. Then her friend surprised her.

"We could seek the counsel of Magus, the wizard who knows the dark realms well. I understand that he offers guidance and support to those such as us who seek to explore the inner sanctum." With these words, Marcelus looked questioningly at Samantha. The warrior contained her smile at this turn of events, asking casually, "How are we to contact this Magus? I hear he's very elusive and cannot be found unless he wills it."

"I think I know where we might find him" Marcelus replied. "Meet me here tonight when the sun is one hour gone. I'll take you there." After paying for their meal, the friends parted.

♥The Wizard Magus

Magus was standing alone in the east tower when they found him, still and silent as he peered into the night sky. Marcelus and Samantha approached cautiously from behind, and stopped while still some distance away. In the dim glow of a solitary torchlight, the wizard appeared to them more a statue than a man. It seemed somehow irreverent to interrupt his stillness and solitude. The companions held back in the shadows, reluctant to intrude.

Magus himself was the first to break the silence. A slight breeze ruffled the hem of his long black robe, and to Marcelus and Samantha it was if the statue came alive. He spoke without turning.

"So...you choose to approach what others would avoid." It seemed as if the old wizard knew what was in their minds before they had spoken a word. "Why seek out suffering in the shadows of the castle when you find comfort in the light of day with your fellows? You were not taught to do this, and it is rarely recommended."

Marcelus knew Magus was testing them. The magician was giving voice to the merchant's own doubts as he spoke. In confusion, Marcelus cast a glance at Samantha, who was apparently stunned by the old man's words. Like Marcelus, she had privately questioned her own motives for exploring the dungeons, when the well-lit courtyards, colorful halls and cozy chambers offered such comfort and security. Turning back to his own reverie, Marcelus wished he had not come to this cold lonely tower so late at night. He reluctantly attempted an answer to the old man's query.

"I find myself facing the same situations over and over in my daily life, as if there is a lesson to learn which I have failed to grasp." The merchant paused and looked down at his feet, gathering his thoughts. "Images from my dreams and quiet musings seem to appear in the world around me, almost as if my waking experience grew from the confusion of my inner realms. Unearthly voices from below are calling to me in the dark of the night, and I am compelled to answer them. I seek answers that lie beyond my fear. I have grown tired of my daily struggles which lead inevitably to naught."

Samantha was next to speak. It occurred to her as she mustered her courage that this was more difficult than much of the warrior training she had already endured. And to think she had looked forward to this!

"I too would like to explore the hidden realms. I have

encountered something in myself that I must understand, and I feel I may accomplish this by descent into the depths. And I have heard the strange sounds at night as well."

Still facing away, Magus smiled ever so slightly as he listened to their honest disclosure. His expression was serious, however, when he finally turned to face the two young visitors. "Why then do you come to me, here in the tower? What you seek is far below in the vast labyrinthine realms of dark mystery and untold stories. How can I be of service to you, and why, pray tell, should I consider doing so?"

Marcelus answered quickly. This was a question he had been prepared for. "Legend has it that it was you who created the thick, heavy blackness that conceals the forbidden realms from the light of day. Without you as our ally, we may never make this journey successfully. I have already tried once and failed. We do not have the power to work against the forces of mysterious wiles."

Pleased with the merchant's response, Magus spoke to Marcelus and Samantha as if he were father, friend and stranger at the same time. "I will help you. And I will get in your way. My assistance is not something that is requested once and granted. I am the magic in your mind--your ally when you honor me and your enemy when you do not. When you become small and petty and allow your fears to consume you, I will be nowhere to be found. In this present moment however, your hearts are true and your mission is worthwhile. You have my favor."

Having reached a good transition point in her story, the old storyteller told her listeners to go away for a while so that she could rest. As the crowd slowly dispersed, Marguerite leaned against the trunk of the old oak that had sheltered them. Letting her eyelids close ever so slowly, she drifted into a peaceful sleep.

Chapter Seven: The Lure of Light

After what seemed only a brief moment, Marguerite stirred, her eyelids parting slightly. She was surprised to see that most of her group had reassembled and were watching her in anticipation as she awakened. Stretching her long sinewy body, she stood and surveyed her audience. The crone smiled inwardly as she saw their eagerness, and invited them into the story with her words.

Walking back to their quarters that night after their meeting with Magus, Marcelus and Samantha felt heavy with the burden of their agreed-upon task. To lighten the mood, Marcelus suggested, "Perhaps a day in Aldea would be a pleasant diversion on the morrow. I have some business to attend to, and we can find amusement in the village plaza."

Samantha seemed pleased with the idea, relieved by the distraction from their daunting task. The two felt almost giddy with a sense of excitement as they spoke briefly of their plans, and said goodnight.

As the sun warmed the morning air on the following day, the companions found pleasure in the color, sights, and sounds of the marketplace of Aldea. Marcelus was known by many of the other merchants, and friendly greetings were shouted back and forth across the thoroughfare as he and Samantha strolled and shopped at a leisurely pace.

On several occasions in the bustling crowd, the pair heard fragments of conversations about a new merchant in town named Chrysalis. This man had apparently captured the imagination and interest of many of the townsfolk.

"I hear he's taken his residence in the old mansion to the north side of town." A lamplighter was gossiping with the shopkeeper where Marcelus was gathering supplies. "No one knows for certain whence he comes, but the rumors have him born and raised in Citadel, the famed and wealthy castle about five leagues to the east. It is said that he bears the gift of light, and brings healing to those who follow his ways. I personally think he's a charlatan, and to be avoided at all costs."

Trying to be inconspicuous in their eavesdropping, the two quickly finished their business in the shop and spoke on the sidewalk. "That's the third time I've heard mention of his name," Marcelus said in hushed tones.

"I know," Samantha replied. "I want to meet him, and learn what is so extraordinary about him."

"Let's find him then, and see for ourselves." Marcelus responded in a serious tone, while secretly admiring the way the light played in Samantha's golden hair. His feelings for her were growing beyond those of friendship, yet he still chose to give no sign.

♥ Chrysalis, Merchant of Light

It turns out that Chrysalis had indeed been born and raised in the magnificent and prosperous Citadel. Some claimed that the story of the divine child had originated there, though the elders of Corazon disagreed and proudly asserted that their own castle had actually housed the divine Serai and her family.

Regardless of the truth about its origins, the divine child story had shaped the destiny of the boy Chrysalis in ways more powerful than he could have imagined. Over the years of his childhood, he heard different versions of the tale from many storytellers.

And yet he never fully received its message.

The only part of the fable that truly interested Chrysalis was the mysterious, powerful and healing light that was said to emanate from the divine child. He was enthralled with the idea of this divine light. As long as he could remember, he dreamed of being divine himself, glowing with inner radiance as had the blessed Serai of the legends.

Chrysalis never paid much attention to the parts of the story that spoke of wounded and frightened children and unsightly half-human beasts. He knew that the outcasts and misfits were sent into the dungeons and that Serai had joined them there. He gave little thought to why this had happened. It just did not seem to relate to him.

The impetuous Chrysalis had secretly thought that he himself was divine, and that one day he would be recognized as such. He indeed did have a natural charisma, and was so physically beautiful that he often drew attention from strangers in the castle.

Being among those who favored fair-haired boy children, Chrysalis' parents fostered his inflated sense of himself throughout his childhood.

So his destiny was thus set in place.

And now the boy had come of age as a man, left his home in Citadel and had established himself as a merchant in the village Aldea near the castle Corazon.

Chrysalis fashioned his services and products to spread the light he had grown to love and cherish. The people found this new merchant and his message to be strange and yet somehow intriguing. Some were even inspired to higher visions of themselves and life in general, and saw him as a minister or prophet. This is exactly what he wanted.

Those who considered him a fraud simply grumbled in the background.

Chrysalis had enjoyed a growing following since his arrival, and was capitalizing on his good fortune in every way he could think of. His secret belief that he himself was the source of the light grew daily. He rarely thought of the story of the divine child any more.

Following directions given to them by the shopkeeper, Marcelus and Samantha made their way through the streets of Aldea toward Chrysalis' home and place of business. They arrived around dusk, as long shadows fell across the large structure before them.

The old mansion was both regal and foreboding in its size and design. Webs of old vines long dead patterned its front walls and encircled columns bordering an entrance far more ornate than functional.

A parchment by the front door indicated that the merchant's shop was just inside, and closed for the day. The note further directed them to a side door entrance where apparently some sort of meeting was being held. Curious to see what was happening, they made their way along a moss-covered walkway around the corner.

Marcelus had to duck slightly to enter the small doorway behind Samantha, and the two took a seat against the back wall of the large, well-lit room. Someone standing in the front of the room was speaking passionately as they entered, and the room was mostly filled with closely attending townsfolk.

The audience seemed to be in a trance, as the inspired young man's words lifted them up into visions of hope, clarity and pure light, away from the murky confusion of their suffering and fear. They were hungry, desperate even, to believe that what he said was true—that they need not suffer any longer; that the light he offered would bring them all they needed to take their worries away.

It was Chrysalis, and he was glowing with the passion and fervor of his visions and emotional intensity. His presence and presentation were captivating, and the two new arrivals were soon in his spell like all who preceded them.

Because of their recent circumstances, the companions from Corazon were far too vulnerable to the power of Chrysalis' message. Being on the verge of their reluctant journey to the castle's lower regions, they were susceptible to influence that would otherwise have passed them by. As the evening progressed, the two were increasingly drawn into the alluring web of the light merchant's charm.

Chrysalis offered them an easy way, a path that required only that they follow his teachings. And the reward he promised was nothing less than lasting joy, health and prosperity.

Lost in blissful illusions, Samantha and Marcelus returned to Corazon transformed and transfixed. Feeling rescued from the daunting task of exploring the labyrinth, they virtually forgot their agreement with each other and the wizard Magus. Weeks, then months passed with no mention of it whatsoever.

Marcelus and Samantha were not alone in their newfound obsession with the merchant of light and his teachings. More castle dwellers were going each day into the village to see Chrysalis, hear his message and buy his wares. They returned each day with much excited talk about the wisdom of his words, showing each other the amulets, trinkets and stones they had purchased in his shop.

♥ Captured by the Light

Marcelus became literally consumed by his fascination with Chrysalis and the images the light merchant's conjuring wrought in his mind. Elated and temporarily free from fear, he spent some time with Chrysalis and his followers each day.

He eventually began to neglect some of his own duties as a merchant. All too frequently now, Marcelus failed to provide sufficiently for his customers who counted on him. Beneath the fervor and frenzy of the new enthusiasm in Aldea, dissatisfaction was growing within the castle Corazon.

Samantha likewise became distracted from her warrior duties as a castle guard. She no longer polished her sword, allowing its blade to become tarnished and dull. Seeing this, her friend Sebastian remarked to her one day, "Samantha, your sword is in poor repair. It is unlike you to neglect it in this way. As a castle guard, I need you prepared and at the ready, with your equipment in good form."

"I really don't have much need of my sword any longer, Sebastian. Now that I have discovered the power of the light through the teachings of the merchant Chrysalis, such things are useless to me. All I need is provided in his teachings." Samantha looked almost drunk as she spoke these words. Sebastian decided not to respond. At that moment, he made up his mind that he would meet this Chrysalis for himself, and see exactly what he was doing to his followers.

As Chrysalis' success and reputation grew, other changes unfolded around him. Although his message and his goods offered healing and encouragement, there were some who felt unworthy, too far away from the lofty language and shining emblems he offered.

Many of the poorest and most infirm of Aldea and Corazon began to retreat farther into the shadows. Ashamed of their condition, they felt unworthy to attend the meetings and they were incapable of buying the goods.

Although the light merchant offered healing and hope, his words and wares were not meant for those most deeply in need.

It was the bright and beautiful, the wealthy and established ones who were most likely to be among the followers of the merchant of light. Despite the many skeptics that dotted the periphery, however, the mainstream townsfolk and castle dwellers were taken with the elixir of luminosity that Chrysalis offered.

Over time, there grew a shortage of food and supplies in the stores of the castle and the village. Many other merchants, like Marcelus, had begun to neglect their duties to acquire and accumulate.

The rumblings grew stronger and louder beneath the floors of Corazon.

Marguerite shifted, leaning forward slightly to let her audience know she was entering a different part of the story.

Her movement caught and held their attention a little more intensely, and her voice was quieter now.

♥ Wisdom in the Forest Home

Deep in the forest outside Corazon, Magus lived in a secret chamber, nestled in the heart of an ancient, massive oak. A passerby would never know it was there, by the wizard's magical design.

Under a star-filled moonless sky, the wizened old man made another of his nocturnal visits to his forest home. As quiet as the shadows that stirred around him, Magus disturbed not a leaf in his way. When the oak loomed over him, he turned his head to the side, and with a slight swishing sound he was gone.

Inside the massive tree, the wizard turned and looked at the plaque that hung crookedly above the doorway. Nearly concealed by a vine that had crept in from outside was a framed inscription burned deeply into a gnarled piece of hardwood. The ancient lettering read,

> The closer you fly to the light
> The larger the shadow you cast

Pondering this age-old wisdom, Magus reflected on what was happening in the castle and village. He thought of how recent movement toward the light was casting ever-expanding shadows into the dungeons of Corazon and the out-of-the-way places of Aldea. It was a process that Magus knew well, having seen it many times in his unusually long life.

Though enjoying the solitude of his secret warren, Magus knew he was not alone. He smiled without looking in the direction of his silent companion.

The large blue-black raven peered at the wizard as he lit his candles.

Sensing the right moment, the huge bird swooped down from his perch to land on the shoulder of the old man. It was a familiar roost for this rare and privileged guest in Magus' lair. The wizard seemed not to notice the arrival of his old friend, as he opened the huge candle-lit book on the chest-high table before him. The words on the page seemed alive in the light of the dancing flame.

> As the outer light fades
> And the inner rumblings grow
> From the heart of the darkness within
> The true light calls us home

♥ False Light Fading

Meanwhile, Chrysalis wasn't sleeping well. Since his success and notoriety had begun to grow in Aldea, disturbing images and events were intruding upon his dreams. All that he avoided in his day moved toward him in the night. Dark, tragic figures of suffering and torment came flooding through the doorways of his nightmares, too many for him to stop. He would always wake at the moment it seemed his mind would snap.

The merchant of light became edgy and irritable in his daily activities. His work seemed a strain, as if he were dragging dead weight. His stories of light and inspiration lacked the energy they once had. Attendance in his meetings began to drop off. The skeptics were showing up to question his ideas, and he found himself getting angry too often. Sales of his products declined. Chrysalis began to doubt the security of his business, and he privately questioned the veracity of his mission.

Restlessness in the shadow realms began to tell on Marcelus and Samantha as well. They tried to ignore the dreams they were having, in hopes that their newfound savior Chrysalis would lift them away without any effort or strain on their part.

It was late on a Saturday afternoon, and Marcelus sat with the sparse crowd in Chrysalis' meeting room. The merchant of light seemed in a foul mood, his message and manner bordering on ranting.

"We must stamp out our darkness and conquer the demons of anger and fear! We must soar into the light together! All those indulging in fear, sorrow and ire will be condemned to eternal misery, exiled from the joy of light forever!"

The look in Chrysalis' eyes was maniacal as he spoke these words, and Marcelus felt compelled to put a stop to what was happening. He was drawn into a desire to change Chrysalis' mind, almost as if his life depended on it. Without thinking about what he was doing or what the implications might be, he stood up suddenly and interrupted the speaker with, "The wounded and the frightened souls have a place in this world too," he argued, "regardless of their state or status. It is the right of each person to receive acknowledgment and respect, however unacceptable they may be to another!" Marcelus surprised even himself with his words. He was not sure where these ideas were coming from, though at moments he thought he sensed the presence of Magus in his mind.

Chrysalis simply ignored the merchant from Corazon, as he did everyone who disagreed with him. He waited for the merchant to finish speaking, and continued with his raving as if nothing at all had happened. This alienated Marcelus far more than any overt argument would have.

After a few weeks of such futile efforts to reach Chrysalis, Marcelus grew so angry that he could not stop thinking about his problem. He was obsessed.

In the middle of yet another sleepless night, He slowly began to realize that he was doing exactly what he was condemning. He had not made a place in his own heart to acknowledge and respect Chrysalis. In the process of trying to change him, he had become just like him.

Deep in the forest concealed within his oak haven, Magus sat on a high stool hunched over the ancient tome. The wizard had observed Marcelus' process through his inner sight, and now smiled to himself. He knew that the merchant had discovered an ancient truth. And there it was on the page before him now.

> If we fight our enemies long enough
> We become just like them

"Wake, up, merchant! You chase your own shadow!" Magus heard himself saying in the deep recesses of his vast and mysterious mind.

In what seemed like a sudden jolt of awareness, Marcelus remembered why he had begun making the journeys into the dungeons beneath his castle. He had not found the answers to his questions in his daily life, and had resolved to look within. He realized now that he had gone astray once more. Following the teachings of Chrysalis was not much different from his quest for gold in the marketplace.

Magus listened quietly to Marcelus' thoughts, approving of the merchant's return to his senses. Pleased for the moment, the old wizard snuffed his candles and moved to more comfortable seating. Lowering himself into the moss-covered chair perfectly suited to the contours of his long,

bony body, the wizard drifted off into the quiet reverie from which emerged his deepest magic.

After a pause, Marguerite blinked and looked around her. In the passion of her storytelling, she had forgotten where she was. It was as if she were waking up from a dream. She saw the listeners around her beginning to stir, and noticed that the night had fallen. She had not intended to go on for so long. Now it was certainly time to close for the day. Smiling slightly, and picking up her small leather bag, she bade the villagers good night, and slowly began her journey back to the castle, followed by those who lived with her in Corazon.

Chapter Eight: Lions at the Gates

Marguerite was sitting on the stone steps of the village temple, on a still, gray afternoon. A small gathering of her listeners began to form, just as the temple bell tolled. It was with some trepidation and considerable anticipation that the wise old crone began the next phase of her story. As she felt the focus of the villagers settling upon her, a soft breeze lifted the scattered leaves in the church courtyard, swirling them gently into a pile at the foot of a stone lion beside the walkway. Smiling softly at this affirmation of her intent, she began to speak.

Legend has it that long before the birth of Marcelus and Samantha, there was a time when many of the dwelling places throughout the land were temples and places of worship. It is said that these temples had been erected to honor the birth of each and every soul as divine, pure and innocent, in connection with the source of being.

Each child born in the sacred dwellings was honored for

her or his natural ability to know and express pure love and joy. All of the activities of the temple residents were for the purpose of providing and celebrating divine connection, and for honoring the sacred essence of each being.

Over the years, experience had shown the temple dwellers that there were dangers round about the boundaries of the temples, which threatened to contaminate the natural beauty and innocence of the sacred life within. It was with this knowledge that living lions and other ferocious guardians were placed at the entrances and gates of the sacred dwellings, to provide safety for those within their walls.

For some time, all seemed to fare well within this system. The ferocious guardians maintained the protective perimeter in order that the vibrant life within the temple could flourish. Only those with pure hearts could enter the sacred space. No one with fear or impure intent could pass the bristling power of the beasts at the boundary.

The temple Serenus, to which our story now guides us, was known for its particularly powerful and vibrant occupants, and for the magnificent lions that were its guardians.

Serenus was a realm of peace and joy, and had been for many years on end.

And then one day, for no reason that any could discern, a spirit of discontent was awakened in the hearts and minds of the temple dwellers.

An unfamiliar story began to move around among the people of Serenus as if it had a life of its own. It told of poor lost souls wandering in the surrounding woods, without a home or a place to rest.

"These disheveled and afflicted ones can gain no access to the temples. Their fear and inner torment allow them no passage by the scrutiny of the lions at our gates, or the beasts guarding any sacred space." It was Cirrus who was speaking, the youngest member of Serenus' high council.

The council was gathered for its regular governance meeting, and Cirrus had the floor. An unspoken purpose of the meeting was to consider the problem of those lost in the darkness outside the temple, and to determine if it was truly a valid concern. Cirrus now presented his argument to the elders seated before him.

The young man was passionate and convincing, as he paced the highly polished floor of the council chambers. "We have enough light and love to share with these lost souls beyond our temple bounds. We cannot simply let them suffer. The problem lies with the guardians at our gates. Being beasts, they are beyond reason and consumed with their purpose. Their function is to protect us from danger, and yet they also prevent the entry of those in need. If we are to offer help to those outside our walls, something must be done to contain or temper the beasts."

A powerful silence followed the impetuous Cirrus' words. No one had ever suggested such a thing, and the elders had no precedent for responding.

♥ Marion and Cirrus

Marion, the senior woman of the council was the first to respond. Known throughout Serenus for her kindness and generosity of spirit, this wise leader shifted in her chair before speaking. An unfamiliar doubt clouded her countenance as she spoke to the passionate petitioner.

"What do you propose, dear Cirrus? The beasts have been with us from the beginning of time, keeping safe our sacred space that we might continually celebrate the joy of divine birth and the pure light of our home." Wisdom and grace were apparent in Marion's demeanor, as she kept an open heart and mind in her inquiry regarding Cirrus' intent.

"I have heard tell of a wizard named Magus who lives nearby in the forest," Cirrus submitted with a little too much authority in his manner. "It is said that he knows spells that bring stillness to the beasts, so that they would pose no threat to those who come and go."

A few of the elders caught their breath. The idea threatened their entire view of the world, yet in their wisdom they knew they must be open to the possibility of change. None gave voice to the outrage surging inside.

"No real harm will come to the lions," Cirrus continued. "I suggest that we allow the wise Magus to help us. We may thus offer aid and solace to those in need without concern for their safety at our own gates."

Cirrus' proposal reflected both his compassion and a desire for new adventure, a combination that would prove dangerous in events to follow. Restless since the spirit of discontent had entered the temple, he found the predictable order and sameness of life within Serenus to be stifling. The possibility of bringing new stimulation to his life was exciting to the restless young man. He looked intently into the eyes of the elder woman Marion now, knowing that his compassionate appeal would speak to her generous heart.

Marion could feel a shift beginning, deep within her soul. Even as she made her decision, she knew that what she was about to do would change life as she had known it, for all time. She was compelled to give her consent to Cirrus' plan, however, feeling a sense of divine destiny speaking softly in the events unfolding. Her words came now from this soft inner voice. There was an unearthly feeling in the room as Marion addressed the council.

"I for one say that we send Cirrus to fetch this wizard, if he be willing to help us. Let us explore this new possibility, and see of what help we may be to those who are lost and suffering." Her eyes moved slowly from one member to the other, coming finally to rest on Cirrus. Each council member had nodded silent consent. It was done.

As Marion slowly left the council chambers with her head uncharacteristically down, she contemplated her life deeply.

She was one of the rare beings who actually remembered her existence prior to birth.

Before the beginning of her life in the temple Serenus, Marion had lived in a spiritual realm of wisdom and everlasting joy. She had existed in the pristine purity of divine grace, where no harm or blemish ever tainted the peace and serenity of those fortunate enough to inhabit those realms. Prior to recent events, Serenus in many ways resembled her former home.

Now she knew this would be no more.

♥ Finding the Wizard

Having received the blessing of the council, Cirrus lost no time in departing the temple. Packing but a few meager provisions, the excited young man set out on his journey to fetch the wizard.

As he sped through the temple gates, the lions on their pedestals turned their magnificent heads to watch Cirrus pass, almost as if they knew what was to come.

A deep rumble rolled within the massive chest of Regalis, the beast to the north side of the gates. His brother Leone likewise sensed an unknown danger. His answering growl was a sound so ominous it seemed to come from the bowels of the very earth itself and shake the stone pedestals on which they sat. Then, all was quiet once again...as they waited.

Their duty was clear, and the noble beasts would not abandon their post.

While passing through a village near Serenus, Cirrus learned of the ritual for seeking counsel with Magus.

A passing minstrel was entertaining a small crowd near the town plaza, and Cirrus stopped to listen for a moment. After hearing a couple of songs, he approached the minstrel.

"In your travels, have you heard of the whereabouts of the great wizard Magus?"

The colorfully clad minstrel smiled and said nothing. Leaning his lute carefully against the sycamore that shaded his performance, he put his arm around Cirrus' shoulder and led him a few paces from his audience. When they had some privacy, he spoke.

"It is said that not all who seek him will find what they seek. The stories tell that Magus appears only to those he feels guided to approach. So, this is what I can tell you."

The bard leaned forward and looked intently into Cirrus' eyes. When he spoke, it was in hushed tones as if the message were for no other ears than his. "Go to the large clearing in the oldest part of the great forest. The age and size of the trees will guide you to the place. Seekers must go there and hold a quiet presence. If the wizard senses a readiness, he will appear. Some have been known to wait for days, to no avail. For others the wizard appears almost instantly. Good journey to you, friend."

With that the minstrel bowed slightly, and returned to his waiting audience.

Cirrus listened to the music and poetry a while longer, then took his leave. He had no idea of the veracity of the minstrel's words, but something about the man led him to follow his guidance as he resumed his quest. He actually had little other option at this time.

The young traveler had no trouble finding his way to the clearing among the ancient trees in the heart of the forest. The bard's guidance was proving true so far, as Cirrus found a comfortable place to sit amid the giant arboreal sentinels surrounding the sunlit, grassy opening.

Accustomed to meditation from his years residing in the temple Serenus, he had no trouble settling into a place of stillness. After several hours, he finally sank into a deep and tranquil meditation. Immersed in peace, all thought of Magus and Serenus drifted away.

And that is when the wizard appeared.

Without knowing why, Cirrus opened his eyes.

Magus was standing before him, though the young man had heard no sound of his approach. "Come with me," were the old man's only words as he turned and walked into the woods.

As if his body had a will of its own, he found himself rising and following the wizard into the dark thicket. When they were but a few meters into the woods, Magus stopped and turned toward Cirrus.

"What you ask is highly unusual," the old man offered upon hearing Cirrus' request. "I have only performed such services when a beloved beast is ill, to preserve its life until a cure is found, or in case of a madness that made an animal unsafe. Your lions are performing their sacred duties, and no harm is threatening."

"What you say is true," Cirrus answered. "Yet, there are many in the forests who need the care and light we can provide in Serenus. The beasts at our boundaries prevent us from offering such care. The threat is to the healing and sustenance of those in need. Surely you can see the value in stilling the lions for a while." Cirrus waited after speaking.

A few moments passed, and the wizard seemed deep in deliberation. After a while he sat down at the foot of an ancient oak that seemed to somehow open and receive his body when he leaned against it. As Cirrus watched the ancient magician, there were moments when he couldn't tell where the old man stopped and the tree started. The moments led to hours.

Finally, the magician stirred, and his eyes found those of his young visitor.

"I will come with you to your temple." With no further words, Magus rose in one fluid motion and began walking.

Slightly in shock and half asleep from sitting still so long, Cirrus struggled to his feet and hurried to keep up with the long energetic strides of the wizard.

The two arrived while the first glow of day's light cast a crimson shade about the temple gates. On their approach, Marion emerged from within the inner sanctum as if she had known the time of their arrival.

The serene, spiritual woman had developed a fondness for the lions over the years, and wanted to insure that they were not harmed in the procedure Magus was to perform.

The lion Regalis and his brother Leone allowed the wizard to pass unmolested through the temple gates. They sensed Magus' noble intent and open heart, which were strong despite his plans.

Inside the temple walls, Marion, Magus and Cirrus discussed

the plan. The younger man, vibrant with the enthusiasm of change and transformation, had more passion for the exchange than did his two elders. Marion and Magus both assumed an almost defeated posture and attitude. It was as if they knew that this thing must occur, but neither one wanted it or was sure that the outcome would be good.

The three talked until there was nothing new to say. When finally Marion was certain that the beasts would not suffer during the process and could be restored to full life, she gave her permission for the magician to proceed.

♥ Turning the Lions to Stone

At the moment of Marion's acquiescence, a hush fell over the forest. The light of the morning sun seemed to dim ever so slightly, though there were no clouds in the sky.

Reluctantly raising himself to his painful task, Magus emerged from Serenus and walked slowly toward the temple gates.

Leone and Regalis turned to look at him as he passed.

As he reached the other side of the two noble beasts, the wizard turned to face the temple and its guardians. He waited in silence. Cirrus and Marion watched from just outside the temple doors.

Just as Cirrus began to wonder if Magus had changed his mind, he raised his arms with his palms facing the lions. He began his ritual with these words:

"You have served us well, noble friends, and we thank you. We have need of a new opening now, one which you would not allow. Let the stillness of sleep take you, that those whom you would not tolerate may pass to receive the healing of the sacred powers within our holy temple. You have valiantly provided your protection for us these many years, and we are grateful. We enter a new era now, in which we will learn and grow, suffer and die, only to be born again. One day we will awaken you from your slumber, that you may know your place by our side once more. Farewell, dear lion brothers, beasts of the field, mighty ones of our soul, may you rest in peace."

Tears streamed from the beautiful amber eyes of the lady Marion, as she tasted the bittersweet power of the moment. Cirrus stared trance-like, as the color began to leave the lions. The life, the warmth, the rich golden glow of their presence was fading. A gray pallor traveled down from the tops of their heads across their regal faces, along their broad shoulders, slowly surrounding their entire bodies until even their sturdy paws were the color of granite. Stone cold and still, the lions at the gates of the temple were statues, mere replicas of what they once had been. Marion was barely able to stifle the voice within her that wanted to cry out, "Oh, what have we done?"

Yet without a sound, she turned and disappeared into the temple, hoping to somehow contain the tremendous sorrow that welled within her.

Pausing a moment before going on, Marguerite looked into the hearts of her listeners. She could feel their confusion and sadness. She gave voice to a question each listener held in his heart, but had not the courage to ask: "Where did the souls of the lions go? Are they dead? Did something leave the beasts when their form turned cold and hard, no longer suitable for their vibrant spirit? If we move back in our story a few moments, and slow down a bit, we may be able to find answers for these questions."

♥ Lost Souls Searching for a New Home

As their physical forms turned to stone, Leone and Regalis' warm, bright spirits slowly departed their now cold forms. Lost and disconnected from their original place and purpose, they stood off to the sides of their stone bodies and looked around in confusion. The lion-spirits watched as Marion slowly returned to Serenus, her head bowed in sorrow. They saw Cirrus standing as if transfixed, in total awe of what the magician had done. They saw Magus lower his head and quietly walk away alone.

In their invisible, ethereal form, the brother lions were dazed and unsure of what had just happened. They only knew for certain that they had lost their sacred place as guardians of the temple.

Holding no anger toward Cirrus or Magus, the two lost souls simply longed to do what they had been born to do. Their mission was to protect the divine order of life, and this was somehow connected to the humans who had always, up until now, honored them and given them a place. Silently looking into each other's eyes for the briefest of moments, they turned and slowly wandered away, along separate paths.

As he made his way sadly through the woods, Regalis felt a deep and powerful longing to return to his rightful place at the gates of the temple. He longed to hear the sweet, hypnotic music from the inner sanctum, and to see the children playing at his feet, safe within his protective gaze. The farther from home he wandered, however, the more these memories faded. Something new and strange grew in their place. A deep stirring slowly began to emerge from within the depths of Regalis' lion soul.

Separated from his honored and rightful place, he was becoming more wild and dangerous.

As he made his way into the darker depths of the woods, Regalis began to sense a presence that was both strange and familiar. The scent was of human, though not like that of the beings that inhabited Serenus. There was a sense of emptiness, a hunger and a longing in the air around him. As the presence grew stronger he stopped, sniffed, and waited.

The lion-spirit did not know that he was invisible. He was surprised to see the shadowy figure emerge from behind a tree to his left and walk within inches of his nose as if he weren't there. Then slowly, one by one, the others appeared before him.

The hapless Regalis had encountered a small gathering of the same lost souls who had been the cause of upheaval in his temple home. Morose, disheveled creatures, they lurked in the shadows behind the trees, and crouched among piles of brush so as not to be easily seen.

For reasons he did not understand, the beast-protector knew he had found a new home. He was needed here. There was no temple to guard, but these were certainly souls in need of protection.

The scent of deep anguish coming from his new companions was strange to Regalis. It was the cause of the growing agitation inside him, which aligned itself with his urge to protect, and to avenge wrongs done.

The forest-dwellers sensed the warmth of the lion's presence among them, and responded with a mix of excitement and fear. Regalis' spirit slowly dispersed itself, entering their hearts and minds and the empty places in their souls. A sense of raw, uncontrolled power permeated each of them. Where moments ago there had been only pain, fear and a deep sense of despair, these lost souls now experienced a kind of wild energy that both empowered them and made them just a little more insane. Their physical and emotional hunger became a dangerous obsession, and they were no longer willing to simply wander in the woods, foraging for sustenance in the meager offerings that their world provided.

When Leone departed from his lion-brother Regalis, he found he could think of nowhere to go but back to the temple. He was drawn inside and to the people there as if by a tremendous magnet, not knowing exactly what he was doing or why.

Once inside Serenus, Leone discovered that he was free to move about undetected, wherever he chose. His loneliness was strong as he wandered the halls and sanctuaries that had heretofore been off limits to his kind.

The magnificent guardian beast had always had a special feeling for Marion, who seemed to him the most pure of the temple dwellers. The great woman had often stopped to stroke his magnificent mane as she passed. He had felt her eyes upon him as the color faded from his form. He knew her pain, and somehow wanted to connect with her through this wounded place.

Like his brother Regalis, Leone found that in his ethereal form he could actually enter the body, mind and soul of all who had a place for him. He soon learned that everyone within the temple had an emptiness he could fill. In their devotion to pure spiritual practice, they had never given vitality to the primitive wildness that laid dormant within them, and that's where the dispossessed beast entered.

Over the following hours and days, Leone slowly dispersed himself among the temple dwellers. He found a particularly vast and beautiful space in the lady Marion, and this became his favorite place to focus his energy. Yet often as he rested there in the body/mind of the wise woman teacher, he felt as if he was being watched. And he was.

It was the wizard Magus who peered at him, the same wizard who had turned his and his brother's bodies to stone.

♥ Stirring of the Beast Within

With a sudden jolt, Leone bristled. Marion felt a rush of energy she did not understand, and suddenly wanted to go outside, away from walls and people. As always, she struggled for control, hoping the urges would soon pass.

The focus of Leone's attention was an image he discerned within Magus. There in the heart and belly of this wizened old man rested a magnificent and powerful beast unlike any the lion had ever seen. Completely calm, yet bristling with vibrant energy, a fierce and splendid dragon lay curled and nested within the wizard's form. For the first time in his lion life, Leone felt submissive. He knew that if tested, he would be no match for this kind of power.

Sensing the problem, Magus began to soothe Leone with his eyes. Slowly the lion relaxed. He began to feel comforted by the presence of the wizard and his formidable bestial ally. As a cub resting against the superior strength of his mother, Leone breathed deep and relaxed.

Marion was relieved to find her anxiety passing. She was surprised to find that she actually felt better now than she had before. Somehow it occurred to her that her relief had come from the wizard Magus. The old man was watching her with the slightest hint of a smile.

Off and on, for days following, Marion felt a stirring deep in her belly and loins. Unfamiliar thoughts and emotions flooded her mind and body for moments at a time. These were sensations that were foreign and even forbidden by the person she believed herself to be. Each time one of these waves of passion would emerge, she struggled to maintain her composure. Time and again, she straightened herself and tightened the muscles of her abdomen to fight against the dark and disturbing sensations roiling within her. She silently resolved that she would die before she would ever act on such wild impulses.

While Marion struggled for control, Cirrus was thrilled by the tremendous power that Leone's energy brought. Unlike Marion, he did not fight it. Being one who had longed for the new and different, and the first to take up a new cause, he eagerly accepted the fierce power that surged within him.

Rising early one morning, Cirrus strode quickly out into the woods without a word to anyone. He was suddenly desperate to find a place to express this newfound passion.

♥ Unleashing Primitive Energy

In the days following his magical transformation of the lions to stone, Magus had chosen to stay in Serenus. He knew there would be an adjustment period, and felt his services may be needed further.

He also felt responsible, and wanted to see what would happen.

Standing apart from the daily activities of the temple chambers, the wizard watched in wonder as the ethereal presence of Leone entered the hearts and minds of the temple dwellers. He had expected something like this, but had no idea he would actually be able to observe the process as it occurred.

Upon seeing the response of Marion and Cirrus however, he became concerned. They had no idea how to use this tremendous energy that now surged within them. And the wizard knew all too well what happened when such power was unclaimed and undirected.

Meanwhile, Cirrus felt more alive in the woods than he had since the moment he was born. He found that he loved to run through the fields, allowing the pulsing energy in his body to express itself. He had no idea why he was doing this, but felt compelled to do so.

Over ensuing days and weeks, he spent less and less time in the temple.

While roaming aimlessly in the woods near Serenus one evening, Cirrus allowed a feeling inside him to have its way.

The new sensations had been with him for a while now, but he had not given full expression to them.

Now he let go, and the primitive energy inside him took over. Using his hands as much as his feet to propel him through the thick undergrowth, he ripped, tore and roared through the tangle of vines and dense foliage in darkest part of the forest. Primal instincts exploded within him. It seemed he had the strength of twenty men...no, the strength of a beast. The exhilarated Cirrus actually imagined himself a lion for a brief moment. He caught a flash of golden fur in his peripheral vision as he ran. Never had he known such wild ecstatic pleasure.

When he finally began to tire from the physical exertion of his energy burst, Cirrus' thoughts returned to his home in the temple. Walking upright now, he could feel the tension growing in his neck and shoulders. He felt a strong inner conflict when he remembered the soft, spiritual life that he and his companions led. A part of him never wanted to go back there again, yet he knew he would. There were his duties, and...well, he did care for some of his fellow temple dwellers.

Distracted for a moment by his thoughts, Cirrus was brought up short by a rustling in the brush behind him. Still feeling the bristling energy of his activated animal instincts, he swung about wildly as if ready for combat. What he saw brought different emotions, however.

Someone was emerging from the undergrowth. Then, one by one they revealed themselves.

It had all begun with them. The lost, outcast and undernourished beings that were the cause of his campaign to turn the lions to stone stood before him now, casting glances at him sideways as if afraid to meet him head on. But something was different about them now. They were not quite as he had remembered them from his previous visits.

A slight edge of aggressiveness, a tense feeling seemed to hang about them. The largest male, who was apparently a leader, looked more directly at Cirrus. A sudden shiver ran up the young temple dweller's spine as he caught the wild gleam in the dark eyes of the disheveled figure. A feeling of kinship seemed to move between them. The pity and compassion Cirrus had felt before was gone, and something warm and familiar took its place.

Though barely aware of each other peering out from behind human eyes, the lion-spirits of Leone and his brother Regalis had connected once again.

Without a word, the forest-dweller thrust something dark and foul-smelling in Cirrus' direction. Recognizing that it was a gift offering, he accepted. The meat was old and had begun to putrefy; yet Cirrus found that this did not keep him from sniffing and tasting it. He was amazed to find that the raw bloody mass that had been offered to him actually seemed somewhat appetizing.

The two squatted where they were, and passed the meat back and forth until it was consumed down to gristle and bone. Slowly, the other forest-dwellers gathered around, grunting and shuffling uneasily in the stranger's presence. All of them wore animal skins for clothes, and smelled wild and foul. Their hair and beards were matted and sprinkled with debris.

But Cirrus was not looking at their attire or hair, or even pre-occupied with their odor. He was captivated by their eyes.

They were so totally alive and present. When one of the forest-dwellers looked at Cirrus, he knew they were fully focused in that act, and seeing deep into his soul. The language barrier seemed irrelevant in these moments, yet his desire to communicate with them was strong.

Over the next few days, Cirrus learned to connect with his new companions, mostly through gesture and sign language. He discovered that they carried the same kind of animal instincts and ravenous appetites for hunting, eating and mating that had recently emerged so powerfully within him. Cirrus felt a deep comfort and peace with these people, unlike anything he had known inside the temple walls.

♥ The Temple Transformed

Marion stood outside Serenus, filling her lungs with clean, fresh night air. As she looked up, the stars reminded her of her spiritual home. She felt so far away from there now. Everything was different in the temple, and she seemed helpless to avert the changes taking place. She continued the deep breathing to calm herself.

Just as some small semblance of serenity was returning to her, a sound in the woods drew her gaze back from the heavens. She watched and waited, as the form of Cirrus slowly made itself known to her in the soft glow of the temple torches.

As he drew closer, Marion noticed her body tensing of its own accord. There was something very different about the young man that was approaching, though she had known him all of his life. His movements vibrated with energy and passion, and the spiritual woman was temporarily captivated by the delightfully dangerous look in his eyes.

Then, snapping out of her trance, Marion suddenly noticed that Cirrus was being followed.

As the forest dwellers approached cautiously behind their new friend, she realized who they were. Sighing and relaxing her body, Marion let go of something very old inside her, and prepared to receive the new arrivals.

She watched as the disheveled crowd carefully approached the stone lions, unsure of their safety.

So, it was happening.

This is what it had all been about. The debate in the temple, the summoning of the wizard, and the transformation of the lions all occurred for this outcome. Yet the great lady felt no comfort, no resolution as this stage unfolded.

Her alarm grew even stronger as the unkempt arrivals passed the stone lions and approached her, yet she voiced no word of protest. After all, she and the council had assented to their entry to the temple, and she knew now that this was all inevitable.

For the first time in her life, Marion knew the emotion of fear. She longed for the peace she had always known and yet taken for granted. Those times were past now, and would never come again.

With a start, Marion felt another strange sensation. It was coming from Cirrus, who stared at her with a look unlike any she had seen in her pristine temple life.

It was lust that she sensed in him. A part of her body that had always been neutral responded excitedly to the man's lascivious gaze, and she was horrified at herself. She secretly liked his attentions, though in her familiar moral sensitivities she was incensed. The people of the temple had always looked to her for an example of decency, and these feelings stirring in her loins were totally unacceptable.

Marion suddenly realized she was scowling at Cirrus, an expression that felt strange to the muscles of her face, as she wheeled around and strode swiftly back into the temple.

Cirrus noticed Marion's response to his lustful leer, and smiled. The prospect of corrupting the holy woman excited him. His guilt was a mere whisper now, squelched by the rumblings and roar of primitive urges and exhilarating passions. He was truly caught up in and ruled by his newfound vigor.

Since the transformation of the lions, everything was different. And this difference was starting to show up in all who dwelled within the temple walls.

Over the following weeks and months, arguments broke out where previously only harmony had prevailed. Many formerly chaste men and women were disappearing into the shadows to commit unpardonable acts of wanton sexual passion.

In a desperate attempt to create order within the emerging chaos, Marion called a council meeting of the elders. Only a few answered her call. The ones who came were those who, like Marion, had fought against the movement of the beast in their souls and were determined to fight against the wild and reckless behavior around them.

Magus the magician was also invited to the meeting. Marion had noticed how the wizard was acutely aware of, and yet unaffected by the goings-on in the temple.

Jeremai, the oldest and wisest of the council elders spoke first. "We are all too well aware of the alarming developments in the behavior of our fellow temple dwellers. Some of you may not be aware, however, that council member Cirrus has been leading unwitting followers into the surrounding wilderness, where they together commit unpardonable acts. He has also admitted, with our reluctant consent, some of the lost and tormented souls who have heretofore never seen our temple except from afar. He seems to feel a kinship with the forest dwellers. Some of our innocent companions are being abandoned out there, and these tattered strangers are being housed inside our walls, adding to our existing and rapidly growing problems. Something must be done, and swiftly."

Marion suddenly remembered her compassionate motivation for consenting to allow Magus to bring stillness to the lions. "This is our doing, brother Jeremai. We agreed that young

Cirrus would receive the lost souls from the forest into our temple, where we could better minister to their needs. Strange as these recent events may be, Cirrus is merely following through on our agreed upon plan."

Her words and message carried little feeling, echoing flatly off the marble walls of the meeting hall.

Devoid of compassion for either Marion or Cirrus, the old man felt something that resembled a deep growl in his chest. Then, giving up to some force within him, Jeremai blurted out in an angry voice, "We have enough problems of our own without taking on more from outside. We are in danger of complete deterioration. This is no time to be offering help to others...we can't even help ourselves."

Shocked by this uncharacteristic eruption from the eldest of the elders, the group fell into a tense silence.

Then, drawing deeply on a powerful resolve in spite of her weakened state, Marion raised her head and straightened her shoulders before speaking.

"Your views are worthy, brother Jeremai. We must look to our need for protection from that which would defile our sacred temple. Our decision has been made, and we cannot turn back. We have opened the gates to allow these strange forces to enter, all for the purpose of compassion and healing. We must now insure that we are not corrupted in our efforts. Rules must be made for our conduct, and these rules must be enforced with a firm hand. Walls must be built to separate those who would lead others astray, and to keep bad influences out of our sanctuary. Strong men and women who have upheld their values must be chosen to guard the walls and enforce the rules. These measures have never been necessary, but our circumstances now require them."

Her heart grew heavy as she spoke, her breath more labored and shallow with each word. Struggling to maintain her composure, Marion looked at her companions, pretending that she was fine.

Everyone seemed to agree with Marion's proposed course of action, and discussion began on how to make it happen. Before adjourning the meeting, however, the elder-woman turned to Magus. "Wizard, have you any advice or insight to offer us? Being from another realm you may have perspective that none of us share."

The tall, gaunt man stirred within his robes and bowed slightly to the noble woman before saying, "Your story has been changing from the moment we met. It must run its course. I only suggest that you look into your own souls for the meaning of what is going on around you. Your greatest risk is to see the problem as only existing outside yourself."

No one in the room appeared to have understood the depth of what he was saying, which came as no surprise to Magus. If they were to choose at this point to look within, it would change the direction of the events in their unfolding saga, which was destined to run its full course before subsiding.

It was not long before the very appearance of the temple began to change. The construction of inner and outer walls blocked the movement of light throughout the structure, casting deep shadows in every direction. The guards and enforcers of rules became more and more plentiful and powerful. Some constructed armored suits of leather and metal to wear for protection in the line of duty. Swords and bludgeons were constructed for use in the most dire of circumstances.

Towers were erected for lookouts to scan the surrounding area, and a moat was dug in the earth outside the outer walls. Soon the sacred ceremonies only occurred in the deep recesses of the temple, and the number of participants began to dwindle. Dungeons were built to hold the rule-breakers, the deranged and those unfit to be out among the common folk.

The temple was being transformed into a castle.

It was well into the night by the time Marguerite reached this stopping point in her story. Someone in the group had gone out earlier in the evening and fetched food to share, so the storytelling had not been interrupted by the evening meal. They were all tired, and it was time now to stop for the day. The crone could feel the sadness of the story hanging about the villagers as they gathered up their belongings and made their way home. Marguerite also found some sadness in her own heart, even knowing that this defilement of the temple was a necessary and valuable part of the story.

Chapter Nine: Into the Labyrinth

Three days hence, Marguerite sat on a small stone stool in one of the courtyards of Corazon. Only a few cubits behind her were the massive oaken doors that led to the underground labyrinth and the dungeons. The eager group of listeners began to settle in around her, ready to hear the next segment of the saga.

Marguerite smiled softly to herself as she felt a faint and familiar rumbling from beneath the stones at her feet. Without commenting on this ominous sensation, she prepared to resume her telling.

The raconteur's thoughts turned now to the task of weaving her story lines together. The images of Cirrus, Marion, Jeremai and the temple Serenus faded in her mind, as she felt Magus and the lion-spirits of Regalis and Leone moving forward with her into this next phase of telling. When the silence of anticipation had grown to an acceptable level among her listeners, the crone began speaking.

The wizard Magus watched in awe and deep humility as the events around him unfolded in the temple Serenus. He had read legends of such transformations, but never before had he directly witnessed the actual process of a temple re-forming itself into a castle. Though he knew the absorption of darkness was natural and necessary to the evolution of the human story, it saddened him greatly to see these great souls moving from peace and serenity into fear, anger and defensiveness.

And now, as with the passing of a silent, strong wind through time, we find this same Magus standing at the north parapet of the castle Corazon. He is virtually unchanged by the many years he has known. Aging is different with such as he, and some say that wizards and wise women actually get younger over the span of life.

Though more than one hundred in his past, the memories of Serenus and its transformation were crystal clear in the powerful mind of Magus as he now sensed the approach of Marcelus and Samantha from across the castle terrace.

The two had only days ago concluded their regular sojourns to Aldea, disillusioned by Chrysalis' failure to meet their expectations. Marcelus found himself once again drawn by the urge to explore the dungeons of Corazon, to find and face the mysteries that lurked in the shadow realms below.

The merchant had discussed these feelings with Samantha, who easily identified with her friend. The young warrior felt changed inside, since leaving her training and pursuing the light and excitement in the village.

♥ Rumblings from the Deep

Restlessness grew in Samantha's soul. Her thoughts were agitated, and she was feeling more irritable each day. Since returning from the last visit to Aldea her dreams had disturbed her sleep, the images sometimes remaining with her throughout the day. The themes were always violent, as she wielded her sword against foe after foe, never quite able to defeat them.

Walking along at Marcelus' side just after dusk one evening, she recounted her nocturnal adventures to her friend.

As Samantha paused in her telling, Marcelus remained silent for a moment. Just as he was about to voice a question, something caught his eye. The merchant stopped and looked around. He had a strange feeling that he was being watched. Samantha seemed on edge as well.

"What's wrong, Marcelus?"

"Nothing. I just had a strange sensation. I'm sure it was nothing. It almost seemed for a moment as if Magus was here." He continued walking.

"I was just thinking of him too." Samantha responded, falling into step beside the merchant. "I think I would like to talk with him again. I feel a strong need for his guidance and wisdom."

After a moment more of walking in silence, Marcelus asked, "So what do you think is the meaning of your dreams, Samantha?"

As Magus watched their approach, his thoughts were of Samantha, and where she was on her journey of discovery. He knew that she was struggling with some powerful forces inside, similar to those of the temple dwellers in ancient Serenus. The wizard was interested in seeing how the young warrior would handle her journey from this point forward.

The two friends grew silent as they rounded a corner and passed through a dark, narrow walkway with high walls on both sides. There were deep shadows—possibly doorways—

on both sides, but neither stopped or looked to see what might be lurking there.

Suddenly, a large form stood before them. Neither had seen his approach or knew from whence he came.

"So, you have come back." Magus spoke immediately and directly, as if this were the most mundane and expected of encounters.

"Your journeys to the outer light have led you to naught, and you have decided once again to seek knowledge of the truth within. Every step you have taken has value. There are no errors on the path. I know your hearts, and my promise to serve as your guide stands if you are willing." The wizard paused.

Marcelus noticed that he wasn't breathing. The silence surrounding the three was eerie. The voice of Magus broke in once again, as if he had been listening to their thoughts.

"Nothing more need be spoken then. We will leave for the lower regions tomorrow evening at sundown."

As quickly as he had appeared, the wizard was gone. Stunned by what had happened, the two bid their good nights to each other with no further conversation.

In their private chambers that night, both Samantha and Marcelus lay awake long, thinking of their strange encounter with Magus and what their journey might hold for them. Awe, excitement and fear pervaded their hearts as they pondered the mystery of the realms they were about to explore. Several times Marcelus fought off the urge to go to Samantha's room and tell her he wasn't going.

♥ Return to the Labyrinth

The next day dawned bright and clear, and Samantha

found herself filled with a new sense of exhilaration as she prepared for her journey. She met Marcelus for a light breakfast of scones and fruit before going out to the field for a workout with some of her fellow warriors. Her desire to hone her skills had returned, and her sword was once again in good repair.

The merchant was not feeling nearly so chipper as Samantha, and chose to pass his day quietly, walking in the hills surrounding Corazon. He felt the need for some time to ponder over recent events and contemplate the adventure he was about to undertake.

Marcelus' dark feelings came from the memories of his first journey to the depths of Corazon. The strange, haunting sound and the image of the beast had never quite left his consciousness. He knew that this was something he had to face, and that until he did it would continue to haunt him. As the merchant went to meet Magus and Samantha, it was with a deep sense of resolve. Yet he felt no joy or enthusiasm for the task that lay in store.

With a look in his eyes that seemed to flicker between encouragement and warning, Magus stood by the doors to the labyrinth and nodded faintly to the companions on their approach.

Marcelus and Samantha waited expectantly before the wizard, hoping for his guidance for the daunting task ahead.

"At times I will be visible to you, there by your side, and at times you will not see me. I will be vigilant as to your cause, and yet you will often be on your own. I am here to challenge as well as to encourage you. I will work with you through your own thoughts and emotions, and at other times you may hear my voice speaking to you as clearly as you hear me now. I am pleased at what you are doing, and yet I suffer from no illusion that your undertaking of this journey in any way ensures its completion. Remember peace and serenity deep within your soul at all times, and you cannot fail. Journey well."

With that the wizard turned and disappeared into the dark entrance to the labyrinth.

Magus knew that the many pathways in the maze were spotted with openings leading to dungeons and chambers of all sizes and shapes. Yet he shared nothing of this with his two protégés. It was through these openings that the warrior and the merchant were to travel now, in the process of exploring their castle's inner realms.

As Samantha followed the old man into the darkness and waited briefly for her eyes to adjust, she felt a ripple of excitement and fear move through her body. Unconsciously reaching for the handle of her sword, she found its sheath empty. Then, with a sigh of resignation, she recalled having set it aside before leaving her quarters. The only sword that would serve her on this excursion was the sharp penetrating focus of her mind. Gathering her energy and directing it toward the dim light she assumed to be the wizard's torch, she moved forward into the darkness.

Marcelus was the last to enter, his mind racing with self-doubt and an all too familiar debate.

"I am a merchant—what is my profit here? Why do I keep coming back when this only leads to more fear? My purpose, my reward lies outside in the world of light and gold, not here in these shadows!"

Even as these thoughts found form in his mind, the darkness of the labyrinth tunnel enveloped him, bringing back his recollection and resolve. The outer world had failed him, its gold and light slipping away and changing to confusion and turmoil. With a heavy sigh, the merchant lit his torch and set his mind and focus to the task before him. He could barely hear Samantha's footsteps in front of him.

Suddenly, Samantha realized she could no longer see nor hear Magus or Marcelus.

Her fear mounted in her body, as a creeping cold moving up from the dank floor beneath her.

As she stopped to listen for her companions, the only sound Samantha heard was the soft passing of her own breath. The silence was huge, pressing in from all sides.

The otherwise brave warrior's heart was pounding, and in her ears there began a slight ringing. At the moment she felt the beginning of terror, a quiet voice spoke from the back of her mind. "What bothers you is not the silence. It is the noise of your own thoughts and the sensations they give rise to. Relax and breathe. Relax and breathe." Grateful for this awareness and puzzled as to its source, she felt the pounding in her chest begin to subside.

Taking several deep breaths, Samantha remembered why she had come—for exactly this—to become more familiar with herself and her inner world. The maze had merely complied by removing all distractions from the outer world so that she could truly listen within.

Standing still and silent, the warrior slowly became aware of an opening just in front of her. As she moved forward carefully, her foot found a descending stairway. Extending her will through the thick darkness, she cautiously made her way down the ancient, worn steps.

On her descent, Samantha noticed a dry, irritating catch in her throat.

She coughed a few times, trying to clear her airways. The

atmosphere was thick, warm and stifling, making it difficult to breathe. She began to perspire slightly, which gave her a clammy, uncomfortable feeling.

To make matters worse, the passageway grew smaller as she descended, as if the walls were moving in around her. At times her shoulders were brushing both sides of the stairwell, so that she had to turn sideways to continue.

Remembering the words, "Relax and breathe," Samantha stopped for a moment to rest and calm herself. It almost seemed that the heavy air had entered her mind, slowing and dulling her thoughts. Feeling exhausted mentally and physically, the young woman squatted as best she could and leaned against the cold, damp wall of stone behind her. Though a strange sleep tried to take her mind, she knew she must not let it. The feeling seemed more a dangerous stupor than sleep. And this was certainly no place for a nap.

Suddenly Samantha was wide-awake.

A movement against her back completely captured her attention. The wall itself was moving. She tried to pull herself forward, but it was too late. She was losing her balance.

What had been a wall now turned to vapor, and Samantha was falling backward, grasping for something to hold and finding nothing.

She landed hard on an uneven surface, and lay there a moment catching her breath. Groping around, she could tell she was on some kind of small rock ledge protruding from a wall. Her left hand found open space beyond the top of her head, and warm air wafting up from below.

Rising slowly, the dazed young woman turned and found that her small ledge jutted out from a wall about half way between the floor and ceiling of a huge open chamber. All of the surfaces in the room were rough-textured black rock illuminated only by the soft glow of a golden light that grew brighter as she gave it her attention.

♥ Samantha's Vision

There, not more than thirty cubits away in a spacious opening on the wall directly opposite Samantha's ledge was a vision the warrior would never forget. Two magnificent, radiant beings were standing completely still and looking directly into her eyes.

Their gaze held her transfixed.

One of the two was seated on some sort of throne, and it was she who first drew Samantha's focus. Her right hand rested on a scepter. Her countenance and bearing emanated a sense of depth, wisdom and power unlike anything the young woman had ever encountered or imagined. It seemed as if this regal being was peering straight into her soul, seeing and accepting all that was there with clarity, kindness and power.

As Samantha's senses filled with awe and wonder, she felt her attention being drawn of its own accord to the other being standing still, straight and tall to the right of the throne. Also female, this powerful figure focused her dark, intense gaze on the young warrior in such a way as to send tremors through Samantha's entire body. In one of her hands was a golden spear, its sharp point aimed toward the heavens. Her other hand lay on the hilt of her splendid sword, sheathed and pointing down.

The feeling that virtually exploded within Samantha was pure unabashed admiration and respect, tempered with the slightest edge of fear in the face of such bristling energy and power. Before her was the image of her ideal. This was the true spirit of the woman-warrior she had always wanted to be.

The voice that spoke now seemed to reverberate all around the chamber, though the lips of neither image moved.

"We are here, and ever have been. We are before you, showing and lighting your way, yet we live inside you and through your history. We are your ideal, your true nature, your destiny and purpose. We will reward, empower and motivate you from within, and we will always be just slightly out of your reach. Our purpose is to take you beyond yourself into the realms of greatness from which you came and which you will one day again call home. The more you remember us the stronger you will become, and the greater our presence will manifest in your life. We enter through your thoughts, and by the force of your will. We are here to serve you."

Everything the young warrior had ever wanted to be was represented in these two images of power, sovereignty and grace. A profound peace was expanding from the center of her being, filling her senses with a warm radiant power unlike any she had known.

Satisfied that she had received their unspoken message, both queen and spirit-warrior turned their eyes downward to the dark pit that separated them from Samantha. Following their gaze, she realized for the first time that other beings inhabited the chamber with them. As her vision clarified in the dim light, she saw that these figures were neither glowing nor magnificent, and were scattered randomly about the floor and along the walls of the chamber. Crouched, cringing and curled in abject terror, these were the wounded and frightened children of Samantha's soul.

As if her focus had increased their volume, the chilling sounds from below slowly began to reach her ears and her heart, stealing the joy she had known only seconds before.

Samantha had no experience with which to gauge such suffering. Deep groaning, plaintive wailing and barely audible whimpering assailed her senses until it seemed that she would burst from the agony. Instinctively, she struggled to close her heart and turn away from this pain that threatened to destroy her.

♥ The Dark Warrior

At that moment, a completely different sound pierced the subdued bedlam from below. A hideously sinister laughter came from a ledge some distance to her left, up a little ways from the pit that now seemed to pull at her magnetically. Shifting her gaze to the source of this chilling sound, Samantha felt her neck and shoulders tighten as a familiar rage warmed her body from deep within.

What she saw was a massive silhouette of what appeared to be a male warrior figure. He seemed heavily armored—though it was difficult to tell whether it was indeed armor he wore or the thick, overdeveloped muscles of his body. He held strange menacing weapons in both of his hands that were foreign to Samantha even with all of her warrior training.

Her entire body went rigid as she watched him turn to face her head-on. His posture was ominous and threatening, and the piercing intensity of his eyes penetrated Samantha's very soul. He spoke when he knew he had her rapt attention.

"Yes! That's it! Turn away from those sniveling, pitiful creatures below. Give your energy to me. I am your safety and your strength. You know me well, do you not? It is I that love the kill, the surge of power that erupts when we destroy the weak, and overcome the would-be destroyers. I have stood by you always, since first you were wounded. I am all you need now. I am steel, I am cold, and I am deadly. With me you have nothing to fear."

His words grated on Samantha's ears and mind like metal on metal. She was drawn to him by his power, which she had felt surging through her all too often. It was he that had taken over in Aldea that day when Sebastian had stopped her from needless violence and mayhem. It was because of him that she had laid down her sword and sought the light in the village. Here he was again. It seemed there was no escape.

Wrenching herself away from the dark warrior and all he represented inside her, Samantha extended her heart once again to the pleas for help from below. The sinister voice again pierced her awareness, this time with more urgency. "No! Don't go soft and be pulled into pity for those despicable brutes! Without my protection, you'll only be wounded again, adding to their numbers and making my job even harder. You are weak and pathetic. Only I can protect you!" Desperate in his attempts to pull Samantha's attention away from the wounded ones, he leapt from his perch into the pit, with no regard for those he might injure in his landing.

"These pitiful ones are worthless! They count for nothing! We would be better off without them." Raising a hideous bludgeon with his powerful right arm, the sinister being began to swing at the helpless souls all around him.

Without a thought, Samantha sprang forth from her ledge, moving directly toward the vicious dark warrior below. At the moment she took this action, the radiant beings from across the pit re-entered her awareness.

Her peripheral vision told her that the queen was now standing alone in front of her throne. And at that instant she felt the bright warrior-spirit entering her body from behind. An exhilarating power now coursed through her veins as Samantha leapt to the floor of the chamber and landed directly in front of her nemesis.

Enraged at the interference, the dark warrior flew into such wild fury that he literally transformed as Samantha watched. His eyes became red, his nostrils flared, the bludgeon became a claw, and fangs appeared from between his slobbering lips. As the now hideous beast raised itself above the young woman, she found herself automatically, even calmly, raising her hand and placing her open palm on its massive chest, where she imagined its heart might be. Her body and mind were infused with a radiant power that was a mix of both love and ferocity at the same time. The energy that infused her left no room for fear.

And now the demonic visage slowly began to morph before her. It seemed to begin melting at the moment of her touch. Not fully understanding why, Samantha heard herself saying, "Come home now, blessed warrior-beast. Your exile is ended. Take your rightful place once again. You are my protector, and I know you are tired from your many years of trying to stop the suffering. Your methods are not working any more, making you more afraid, furious and frustrated. You have served me well. I will help you in your job of protection, so that you can rest."

As she spoke these words, Samantha beheld the unfolding of a new vision before her. Where the half-human beast had been was now a majestic lion, who looked somehow vaguely familiar. As she opened her arms and heart to it, the beast merged with her very being, bringing with it a warm and powerful sense of balance and wholeness. Now the essence of the dark warrior was hers, returned to its rightful place in the service of truth and justice.

At the same moment that the lion spirit merged with her body, Samantha heard a horrendous series of screeching, tearing, ear-splitting screams.

Moving out from behind the lion, she could see an image of the dark warrior, with something flying out the back of its head. As the pure, sacred spirit of the protector continued to merge with the young woman warrior, her vision showed her glimpses of bizarre, sinister winged creatures flittering chaotically into oblivion.

The soul-wrenching sounds of the winged beasts slowly faded, and with them they took the heavy thickness of the air. A fresh sweet scent began filling the void.

The darkness seemed somehow nurturing to Samantha now, as her attention was drawn to something pulling gently at her tunic. Dreamlike in her movements, she looked down.

Marguerite could see that she had complete command of her listeners' attention, and was certain they would stay all night if she kept talking. She could also see that they were tired, and decided to give them a break to stretch their legs and have a morsel to eat. With mixed reactions of disappointment and relief, the villagers and castle dwellers rose and wandered away, knowing from the past storytelling sessions that they had about an hour before the crone would resume her tale. The old woman herself felt strangely energized, and chose to walk up among the castle towers and survey the countryside from that lofty vantage. As she began her ascent, the thought was strong in her mind of how good it always felt to honor the lost warriors and embrace the beasts. She was looking forward to the next part of the story, the blessing of the children.

As she resumed her story in the soft light of late afternoon, Marguerite felt warmth growing in her heart over what was to come. Being one who is unafraid of sorrow, the wise old woman greeted the prospect of embracing the wounded as an opening to the creative power of love.

♥ The Precious Child

Looking down in response to the tugging at her tunic, Samantha adjusted her eyes to focus on the dark images beneath her. What she saw opened a place in her heart that had not been touched since she herself was small. The wide, staring eyes of a tiny female child reached out and pleaded with her, silently asking for her care and comfort.

As she bent down and extended her arms to the emaciated urchin in rags at her feet, she felt the power of the lion, the presence of the warrior and the vast, magnificent love of the queen surging within her. She knew it was only through the aid of these splendid beings that she was able to face the pain and devastation of the child who was nestling now into her warm embrace.

As Samantha held the frail body to her breast, images and scenes from her own life began to emerge before her. Opening her heart to the sorrow and despair of the wounded child gave rise to remembering. Moments in her childhood when she had been rejected and abandoned by her father flashed before her now, releasing all of the emotions that had been locked away inside them. Deep, empty chasms opened within her, showing her the places where love was needed, and yet had never been. She fell to her knees on the stone floor of the chamber, holding and rocking the blessed child in her arms.

In its midst, her grief seemed to have no end. At one moment, she felt that she was grieving for all children of all time. The entire world's pain and suffering seemed to be right there within her, as if she could reach out and touch the very heart of it.

At the moment when she felt she could bear it no longer, relief began slowly seeping in. Remembering the fragmented and dissociated pieces of her life brought deep, healing sorrow and a growing sense of expansive joy and love. Waves of warm, bright healing energy washed across her heart and mind, filling the emptiness and easing the pain of her many and varied wounds. She could tell that this healing was coming from the child in her arms and in her heart. Samantha was experiencing reunion with the divine child of her soul.

As if awakening from a dream into a dream, Samantha gradually became aware of where she was. As she looked around, she found that the scene had changed. The walls and floor of the dungeon were infused with a soft glowing light that seemed to caress everything it touched. She sensed the magician in her mind, the lion in her loins, the woman warrior in her body and the queen throughout her being. Lifted up by the spirit of power and love within and all around her, she found herself returned lightly to the ledge from which she had leapt into the pit.

Magus the magician chose this particular moment to speak in her mind, saying, "You have done well, my daughter. You have accomplished what you came for, though your work is not yet complete. There are many more wounded ones, who await your return. But go now, and learn to care for this precious one in your arms, that she may be healed by your love and that you may know the healing she holds for you."

Samantha was suddenly filled with a powerful mix of emotions. She could still see the eyes and faces of the frightened and wounded children she was leaving behind, and her heart reached out to them. She had seen them and felt their wounds, and she would not forget.

Though reluctant, she knew she must leave. The work remaining to be done in this place was beyond her capacity at this moment. The voice of Magus was right...or was that her own wisdom speaking in her mind? She was not sure. No matter, the young woman-warrior knew she had plenty of time for such questions.

For now, her attention was irresistibly drawn to the little girl nestled against her breast. She could feel the sweet insistence in the tiny hands that held her so tightly. Samantha savored this moment of connection, while knowing that it would pass. As she walked slowly back up the staircase into the light of the castle courtyard, the image of the child in her arms began to fade. Their reunion was strong, however, for she could still feel the tiny one's presence in her heart.

Without another word spoken, the crone folded her belongings into her cloak and smiled softly at her listeners. As if embraced by invisible arms of love, the small group looked at her with peace in their hearts. There seemed to be some kind of soft, ethereal music playing about their ears, as they silently moved their separate ways in search of rest.

Chapter Ten: Gold in the Shadows

When Marguerite arrived once again in the castle courtyard, most of her regular following had already gathered. They seemed to have known she would return to the same spot for the next part of the story. The wise old storyteller quietly arranged herself to begin, pleased at the growing sense of connection between her and the loyal listeners.

As he watched Samantha's form being swallowed in the darkness, a sudden flash of awareness leapt into Marcelus' mind. "Buried treasure," he surprised himself by speaking out loud, though still quiet enough that none could hear. It occurred to him that there might indeed be gold on this journey after all, if any of the old legends were true. His fellow merchants had often passed the time over ale in the evenings with stories of riches hidden in the depths below Corazon. No one knew the veracity of these tales, but the mere possibility was enough to spur Marcelus forward on his otherwise reluctant path.

Renewed in his energy and enthusiasm, the merchant pressed onward into the unknown realms ahead.

It was not long before he, like Samantha before him, found himself alone. The heavy thickness of the air pressed in on him from all sides. It almost seemed to be alive, like it wanted something from him. He tried to put these thoughts out of his mind, but they would not go away.

Then the skin on the back of his neck began to tingle. In his growing anxiety he imagined that he could feel small insects crawling on his body. The more Marcelus focused on these sensations, the more pronounced they became. His breathing became shallow, and he began to think of turning back...out of fear...just as he had in his last aborted attempt to brave these regions.

"I can't let this happen again," he thought, "I have to find a way past this!" His inner dialogue seemed to ease him somewhat, activating a determination he had often used to negotiate challenging situations. The young merchant had learned well to talk himself out of vulnerable feelings, like his father before him.

As soon as his attention moved back to the irritating feeling on his skin, however, his fear escalated even beyond where it had been before.

The old coping skills just weren't working any more.

Magus knew he could not reach the merchant through his mind. He had made several attempts to do so, as he watched Marcelus work himself into a panic. But the wizard's soft, insistent voice could not be heard over all of the clatter and chatter of the young man's racing thoughts.

Magus decided to take on his invisible form and slip into a side chamber of the labyrinth. He had hopes of weaving a vision that would not only calm the misguided merchant, but begin the learning he had come to attain.

Marcelus could not believe his ears—music—a woman's voice! Such a sound was the last thing he expected to hear a hundred cubits into the interior of the labyrinth.

The light, soothing sound attracted the merchant as if it was made of tentacles, reaching out and drawing him in.

The sensations on his skin had subsided, though Marcelus was far beyond noticing that subtle change now. His total attention was captured by the sweet sound of the maiden's voice, as she sang her strangely soothing melody.

Intoxicated by stirring passions, Marcelus impulsively entered one of the openings to the maze. The music wafting in the dark tunnel pulled him even further onward despite his fear and sense of helplessness. Some part of his mind was still telling him to turn back, yet a force drove him that was stronger than reason.

A dim light appeared in the tunnel, and the music grew louder. The more he progressed, the clearer the voice and the brighter the light. His heart pumping with excitement now, he knew only that he must discover the source of that ethereal sound.

At last, there she was. Dazzling in the golden light, a maiden sat on a gilded throne, surrounded by treasures beyond imagination. The merchant had never seen anyone so totally captivating in her beauty and allure. She had stopped singing now, and her moist eyes were open toward him in what seemed to be anticipation and desire. His eyes drifted from her slightly parted glistening lips to her ample breasts partly exposed within the regal satin gown she wore.

This vision represented a culmination of everything Marcelus had worked for and desired throughout his entire life. This was the gold, the buried treasure that had spurred him along his journey. This was the beauty and the passion that were his secret heart's desire. It seemed he was near exploding with emotion, as he came closer to the beautiful enchantress and the abundant wealth that encircled her.

Standing before the maiden now, Marcelus could not resist the urge to reach out toward her. As soon as he lifted his arms in her direction, however, the glorious apparition before him began to change. The beautiful form of the maiden faded, and the gold lost its luster.

The image morphed into that of a hideous hag, whose hungry eyes reflected the same greed and desire he felt for the maiden and her gold.

This despicable creature was reaching impatiently for him now, as if she wanted to devour his body and soul. Marcelus felt such terror and revulsion at the sight before him that he could not move. Frozen in fear, he felt her claws digging into his arms and shoulders, as a scream began to erupt from the deepest realms of his being.

The sound ripped and tore its way out of his throat, like something wild and frantic escaping from a deathtrap. The wrenching sound that came from the merchant seemed to have a life of its own. As it emerged it opened regions of his soul he had not known. It seemed to have no end.

When finally the guttural cry subsided Marcelus returned to himself exhausted, as if waking from a horrifying dream. The awareness slowly dawned on him that this was the same sound that had stopped him in his tracks on his ominous first attempt to explore the lower regions of Corazon.

The merchant's entire body was as cold as ice, and yet he was covered with perspiration. The apparition had completely vanished, and he was left only with his terror. Dizzy, he reached out for something to lean against, and found the hard, reassuring wall of the tunnel within inches of his arm. As his breathing slowed and his muscles relaxed, Marcelus had the feeling he was not alone.

"Your vision has gone deep, my young friend."

The familiar sound of the wizard's voice was comforting to Marcelus, as he turned to the tall presence behind him.

"You have done well, although your journey is not complete. What you have seen holds the truth of your struggles, though at this moment it leads you only to despair. When you dwell quietly in this rich place, you will move beyond to a grander vision that reveals your ultimate journey. What you saw dwells within you, and will reveal itself repeatedly in your life until you receive its lesson. The answers you seek also reside within, and can only be reached by a silent settling into the feeling of each moment."

As the last of his words sank into Marcelus' mind, Magus turned and began his ascent from the labyrinth. Distraught and devoid of energy, the merchant hung his head and followed, knowing that he had nothing now but the words of the wizard to guide him. As he wearily dragged his tired body up the seemingly endless staircase, he heard the light footsteps of Samantha behind him. Relieved by the presence of his companion, he felt some energy entering his body. The thought occurred to his tired mind that she might be able to help him along the next leg of his journey.

At this point, Marguerite rose and stretched her long and ancient body, grown stiff with the time of sitting. Looking around at her gathering of villagers and castle dwellers, she smiled with compassion and sympathetic concern for their well-being. Many looked troubled, lost in contemplation of the questions that the story had raised in their hearts and minds. In contrast, a very few looked strangely content. These she knew had moved beyond Marcelus' struggle in their own stories.

"Let the pieces of the story that grabbed your attention have their way with you for a while. Then let them pass. Hold to nothing. Follow the advice of the wizard to Marcelus and reside in the feeling that is in you. It has a truth it would reveal, and you will do well to allow it. Go to your homes, your labors, and your play, while keeping a sacred place in your hearts for the story to work its wisdom. We will gather again in a fortnight, and see where our tale will take us. Until then dear ones, be well."

Without a word spoken among them, the tired and thoughtful group dispersed, returning to their respective lives, which were somehow more interesting and intriguing when seen against the backdrop of the crone's emerging story.

♥ Marcelus Finds True Gold

Knowing the listeners were eager to hear the next segment, Marguerite sent word out early that their next telling would be in the castle counting chambers.

The familiar glint of greed and lust for gold was quite evident in some of the castle dwellers' eyes as they entered the counting chambers and found their places around the large, spacious room. Few of them had ever been inside this part of the castle, and knew it was only with the sponsorship of Marguerite that they were permitted to do so now. Most of the store of the castle treasures was locked away in a secret hold, to which only the castle chamberlain could gain access. Mere proximity to the glistening stacks of coins and bags of gold was enough, however, to spark the interest of all those present for the crone's story. When the last of her listeners was settled, she began.

It was deep into the night, several days past their excursion when Samantha heard the soft knocking at her bedchamber

door. As the familiar voice of Marcelus came from the other side, she quickly undid the latches to allow him entry. Before her friend said a word, she could feel the heaviness of his mood. His head hung low, the merchant made his way across the cold stone floors to slump into a large chair by her bed.

Her room cold for sleeping, Samantha tossed Marcelus a bearskin wrap and stirred the few remaining coals in her fireplace. Snuggling back under her covers, she asked, "What brings you out so late on this cold night? Are you not well?"

"I have not slept in three nights" he replied in a voice heavy with fatigue. "I am caught in the web of my vision. I can't escape my longings any more than I can find relief from my fear. The wicked hag came to drive me away from the dream of my heart's longing. Right there, within my grasp, was everything I have ever dreamed of, worked for and sought after. I must go back, and yet I cannot. The repulsive horror of that hag sinking her claws and teeth into me makes me wish for death itself as an escape."

"I think I know the feeling," Samantha said in a serious voice, looking down. She was remembering her encounter with the dark warrior, and the strength of her desire to kill him.

"What do you mean? How could you understand? You had such a wonderful experience down there you came out glowing. My experience left me barely alive, and I feel that way yet. You know nothing of my journey, so make no assumptions."

Marcelus' tone was peevish and angry, but Samantha took no offense. She went on to provide a more detailed account of her experience in the dungeons, knowing that her friend would understand better after hearing. By the time she was through, the morning sun was bringing a soft red glow to the dim light in her chambers.

Samantha shed a few tears during the telling of her tale, and

Marcelus for the moment was lifted from his gloom by the warm light of compassion for his friend.

After an appropriate silence to honor Samantha's story, he said softly, "Do you think I am to embrace that hag as you embraced the dark warrior? I cannot imagine myself doing such a thing! Surely there is another way."

"I don't know," murmured his friend, "but that certainly seemed to be the lesson of my experience. Apparently the power of the embrace, if done in the right spirit, is great enough to transform the beast into something more palatable and easy to accept. I never could have done it without the help of the bright woman warrior-spirit who came to me at that moment. Perhaps if you can make the first steps toward the proper embrace, it will invite the help you need in order to complete the transformation, as it did with me. I know of nothing else to suggest. Unless...wait! Marcelus! You said you could not imagine yourself doing that. Do you remember the time Magus told us that if we could imagine ourselves doing something it would make it more likely that we would in fact be able to? He even said that in some cases imagining yourself doing something was the same as actually doing it! What do you say? It may be worth a try!"

Catching Samantha's enthusiasm, Marcelus felt some sense of hope for the first time since his return from the dungeons. "I am willing to try it. I can't go on like this much longer, and imagining the journey sounds better than actually going back there. Will you sit with me while I do it, Samantha? Your presence reassures me." "Yes," she answered. "And it may even be helpful if you tell me what is happening as you see it. It's up to you, I just want to help."

Settling more deeply into his chair, the weary young man closed his eyes. With some difficulty at first, he pictured the entrance to the dungeons before him. Slowly, the image became clear. At the moment he thought of entering, his movement through the passageway began. He suddenly became aware of the presence of the wizard beside him...or was he just ahead a ways? At any rate, he was glad that Magus was near, as the merchant was sure to need his guidance on this journey.

Making his way through the winding passageways, Marcelus was beginning to remember the way to the chamber of the maiden. At the same instant, he found that he was already there.

"In this realm, you need only intend an action for it to occur," came Magus' voice, explaining why everything was happening so easily.

"Magus is here," Marcelus told Samantha, "and I am already in the chamber where it all happened."

There was no sign of the beautiful maiden, and what remained of the treasure made only a soft glow of golden light in the shadows. The silence was suddenly broken by a ghastly sound.

"So, you're back, deary!" It was the piercing, screeching voice of the hag coming from the heavy darkness in the corner, a sound as hard on the merchant's ears as her appearance was on his eyes. "You'll not find your beloved princess here, my little whimpering whelp, you chased her away with your pathetic screaming."

"It's the hag," Marcelus reported to Samantha, though she and her bedchamber seemed far away by now. "She's calling me names and ridiculing me. I can't see her, though."

"Try asking her to show herself," Samantha suggested softly, not wanting to interrupt her friend's journey. "She really is trying to help, but she won't admit it." Samantha was surprised to find that she could imagine every part of what

Marcelus was seeing, though she had no idea at all whether or not it matched his perception.

"What are you afraid of, old woman?" Marcelus was feeling more courageous now, empowered by his previous journey and the support of his friend. "Come out and show yourself!"

The surprising fury of the hag was white-hot in intensity, as she came shrieking out from the shadows to hover dangerously close to Marcelus, teeth bared and claws poised to strike. Fear rippled all over the young man's body, but deep inside he could feel the comforting wisdom of Magus and the friendly support of Samantha. When he spoke now, his words surprised him, as if they came from some hidden part of him that had never spoken before.

"It's time to come home, you poor, lost soul. I know that your fury is fed only by your fear. And I know that your purpose is to protect me from the hazards of love and riches and all the ways I can be hurt in their pursuit. Thank you for your efforts, and thank you for showing yourself to me. You have worked hard to keep me safe from the pain of exposure to the gifts of romance and wealth, and I know you are tired from your efforts. You can rest now. You are no longer alone in your efforts to protect me. Your time has come to be rewarded for your efforts with a long rest." As he spoke these words, Marcelus was surprised to feel his arms opening wide to the hag, as he moved toward her with a sense of resolve unlike any he had known.

♥ The Power of the Embrace

What happened in the next few seconds would be a teacher for the young merchant the rest of his life. As he embraced the hag, she transformed before his very eyes. The image became that of a tired old woman relieved at being seen, understood and nurtured. She collapsed into his arms, immediately going limp. She indeed was exhausted and in need of rest.

Thinking of where the old woman would feel the most safe and nurtured, Marcelus imagined a place that was perfect for her needs. Gently and lovingly, he laid the tired figure in a forest bed of pine needles, under the protective gaze of some ancient guardian trees. She was safe and comfortable there, and he could watch over her as she slept.

As Marcelus was basking in the sense of relief that followed these images, he found himself back in the underground chamber in the labyrinth.

Instantly, a movement caught his eye from a dark corner of the stone room. As his vision adjusted, he could make out a pile of dirty old rags scattered about. Something was moving beneath one of the rags. A chill ran up Marcelus' spine. He approached cautiously, afraid of what he might find stirring in that shadowed nook.

As the merchant carefully lifted the soiled shreds one by one, a tiny form was revealed.

With great wariness, the dirty, emaciated boy slowly looked up at him. The child's huge, hollow eyes captured and held the merchant's attention. The mixture of pain and emptiness Marcelus saw there seemed to open a deep chasm in his own soul.

Marcelus was frozen, unable to move closer or farther away.

Magus spoke from somewhere inside him, saying, "This too must be embraced. These eyes are windows to a hole in your soul, which can only be filled with love. This is the child who was never seen, acknowledged or loved. You are the only hope he has. Do what you must do."

As if there were no other choice, Marcelus opened his arms, his heart and his mind to the gaunt, cringing child that housed those enormous gaping eyes.

Holding the boy-child to his breast opened Marcelus to all of the pain that he had felt under the harsh, rejecting, judgmental eye of his father. Even deeper was the pain of not being held, nurtured, played with and acknowledged.

The love he was able to give to the child in that moment washed into those old wounds of emptiness, bringing healing grief and sweet relief. He knew now that the child was an image of himself, giving him a picture of the deepest realms of his pain.

As this healing occurred within Marcelus, he again saw a brief image of the maiden and the treasure. He now understood that these had been but images of his own inner value, which he had sought compulsively in the outer world. The emptiness he had sought to fill with riches and love was the emptiness in the child's eyes. And those eyes were filling now, with tears of love and joy.

Samantha watched as Marcelus wept in her chambers. She somehow knew his tears were washing the wounds of the child, though he had not spoken aloud for some minutes now.

As the merchant's love flowed into the little one, its image began changing. The child now appeared more nourished, and somehow brighter. Its eyes showed the beginnings of peace and contentment, though clearly more healing was needed.

Then something very interesting happened. As if he had been strolling by on a sunny afternoon, Marcelus' father Hector appeared in the merchant's field of vision.

Hector smiled. The feeling that passed between them spoke volumes of resolution. Marcelus realized he was seeing the very best of his father, who wanted only his well being. Slowly, the image of the older man faded.

In the peaceful silence that followed, Marcelus felt himself washed in warm feelings of love and forgiveness. These healing sensations seemed to come from deep within him. For a moment, he imagined that he could see into their source. Staring into the depths of his soul, he found revealed before him a world so beautiful, vast and rich that it created a profound sense of reverence and awe.

The magnificence and power of the multidimensional vista that opened before him now flowed into all of the untouched realms of his being. The majesty and the mystery of pure, innocent love illumined and healed the dark realms of confusion and shame he had carried.

♥ The Child of Light

A new image slowly formed itself in the center of Marcelus' field of vision. It appeared to be a small child, surrounded by a soft, radiant light. The merchant knew who it was even before he could make out her features. As the lines of the face and body became distinct, his feeling was confirmed.

The divine child of legend stood before him. The merchant had never seen the famed Serai, but he had no doubt that this was she. The warm glow that radiated from her somehow eased his pain and brought comfort to every aspect of his being. As he let himself sink into Serai's sweet and innocent gaze, he began to understand his mysterious journey.

Serai spoke not a word, yet in his mind Marcelus heard her say, "All things work together, creating the colorful tapestry of life in its radiant richness and diversity. Be at peace. Embrace the totality of yourself and life around you, and you will remember who you really are and who you were born to be." With her words, Marcelus felt a wonder-filled mixture of release and relief.

He was laughing and crying at the same time.

As these feelings began to subside, Marcelus once again became aware of his physical presence in Samantha's chambers. His body relaxed and his breathing returned to normal rhythms. Then the merchant began to feel a powerful surge of warm, vibrating energy released from deep inside.

Something had come home, and something had departed, leaving him more whole, complete and somehow renewed. Opening his eyes, he saw his friend calmly watching him. She smiled softly as their eyes met.

"You don't have to talk about it if you don't want to. Tell me if and when you're ready," Samantha offered in spite of her curiosity. Grateful for the permission to be silent, Marcelus rose and slowly walked toward the door.

Before closing the door behind him, the merchant paused and turned.

"Thank you," was all he said to his friend.

Sitting quietly for a moment after he was gone, Samantha thought of how different Marcelus looked following his experience. He had an air of strength, power and masculinity about him that was beyond what she had seen in him before. At that moment, she found herself extremely attracted to this courageous man. She smiled to herself as the warm sensations moved through her body.

Like Marcelus, Marguerite did not feel like talking any further. She wanted to savor the feelings the story had stirred in her. There was a familiar sense of peace in the wise old crone, and, pausing a moment, she said a quiet prayer of gratitude for all that had been given her.

Chapter Eleven: The Castle Citadel

Marguerite was ready for a new movement in the story. With no words of preview of what was next to come, she dismissed her audience from the merchant's counting chambers with the invitation for them to join her the following afternoon in the castle courtyard.

Approaching her destination the next day at a leisurely pace, the crone's eyes were drawn to the heart of the courtyard. A warm easterly breeze played there among the leaves of the massive oak tree that was its centerpiece. Families and friends often gathered here to visit and swap pleasantries, especially in balmy weather such as this pleasant afternoon provided. Nestling herself comfortably into an armchair-shaped nook between two large rounded roots of the friendly oak, Marguerite waited as the last of her listeners found their places around her. A silent anticipation arose within the gathering. And she began speaking.

♥ Chrysalis' Story

Growing up in Citadel had been easy for Chrysalis. Favored for his gender and his extraordinary appearance, he gleaned special treatment from all who knew him. With classically handsome features, excellent physical proportions, light auburn hair and an exceptional brightness to his countenance he seemed almost god-like to many.

The effect this had on him was subtle, and yet nonetheless powerful for its subtlety.

Chrysalis was particularly influenced by his parents' treatment of him. Over time, their spoken and unspoken message to him was, "You are different from the others. You are better than they are, more important. You have something they don't have. You have more light and beauty than they do. Who you are and what you do is blessed, simply because of your exceptional qualities. You do not have to suffer like the others. You are exempt from that."

And because many of these messages were silent, they were all the more powerful in shaping the young Chrysalis.

Citadel was a castle where the story of the divine child was even more powerfully upheld than in the castle Corazon. Its lessons were spoken and taught diligently in all of the schools and places of worship. This was a great source of pride for Citadel's leaders.

Quite understandably, when the boy Chrysalis first learned of the journeys into the underworld to retrieve and spend time with the wounded and the weak, he did not want to go. He had learned that the journey through the darkness was the only true path to reconnection with the divine child, yet somehow he believed that this did not apply to him.

Secretly, Chrysalis felt that he was a sort of divine child in his own right. This perception was reinforced by the special treatment he received. As a function of his privileged status in the family, his parents allowed him to maintain his illusions and avoid the journeys he considered to be beneath him.

Little did they know how greatly this would affect him in later life.

The boy Chrysalis had become confused in his thinking as a result of the way that he was raised. He grew judgmental and disdainful of those he considered to be beneath him, and often scoffed at their struggles and suffering. He never considered himself to be in the wrong. Whatever problem occurred, in his mind the cause was outside himself.

He had tasted the illusory power of superiority projected onto him by those who saw him as special. By giving him this elevated status, his friends and family unwittingly gave some of their own light and goodness to him. Chrysalis became intoxicated with the resulting sense of unreal power, which was not truly his to claim.

The boy was completely without the humility that would have required he face his frailties. The possibility that he had limitations never occurred to him.

As he grew more and more glorious in his own mind, it became difficult for others to be with him, and for him to find comfort in their presence.

"He never seems to want to be with the other children. I can't say that he really has any friends. Do you think we should talk to him?" Chrysalis' mother Roberta was putting the finishing touches on an evening meal as she queried her husband.

Chrysalis' father Samuel replied, "He will find his own way. You know he is not like the other children. If he needs their company he will seek it out. We can trust him to make these decisions on his own. Besides, I just don't think he needs the trivial social contact that the rest of us do. He is special, and we must honor his way." Samuel hardly looked up from his task of woodcarving as he spoke.

"Perhaps it would be better if he was more like the other children. I worry about him being so isolated and alone." Roberta fussed with the potatoes as she spoke, as if it were their fault that her son had no friends.

"Just don't let him know you have these thoughts," Samuel answered, with an edge of command in his tone. "We don't want him to think we doubt him. Remember how angry he gets when we question him."

Roberta spoke no more to her husband on the subject. The male superiority in their family was clear and strong, and she knew better than to push too hard against it.

Her worries continued, however, and with good reason.

Chrysalis soon found his thoughts turning away from his home, his family and Citadel. Though many seemed to adore him, no one really knew who he was. Sometimes he realized that no one really wanted to be with him—but he would never admit these thoughts to anyone.

Feeling less and less of a tie to his family and community, the boy began to plan for a time when he would leave Citadel to seek his fortune.

The afternoon shadows of the oak tree grew long and deep, as Marguerite paused to pass the waterskin among her companions. Pulling her shawl a little tighter around her ancient shoulders, the crone smiled at the synchronicity of the deepening shadows with the mood in the next part of the story. Sensing their readiness, she turned back to her small audience and resumed her tale.

♥ Priscilla, Child of the Shadows

By the time Chrysalis' sister had five or six years behind her, she had become painfully aware of her brother's privileged status. Villagers and castle dwellers had been known to comment that young Priscilla lived in her older brother's shadow; with no inkling of the truth they spoke.

In proportion to the status of her brother, Priscilla was seen as having little worth and value. Just as his actions were automatically defined as good or right, her behavior was all too often labeled wrong or bad. Where he received special privileges, she was greatly restricted in her freedoms.

Having received these unspoken messages since the moment of her birth, Priscilla naturally tended to hold her head down and shy away from overt encounters with others. She appeared plain and unattractive, yet in truth she was neither.

The entire culture of Citadel revered males over females. The bards and ministers even took poetic license in making the divine child a male in their songs, stories and teachings. Sons were generally considered to be an asset, and daughters were often seen as mere chattel.

By the time Priscilla began to recognize these discrepancies and the injustice within her family, the effects had already taken hold. Her parents were never overtly unkind to her, but she was never truly valued as a person.

Feeling rejected and disdained in a covert and yet devastating way, Priscilla retreated into the comforting concealment of the shadows at every opportunity. Her bedchambers were beneath the floor of her family's quarters, in a room without windows or fresh air. Although she felt the disdain of her relegation to the darkness, she found comfort in being invisible to those who might otherwise judge her.

By contrast, Chrysalis' chambers were large, open and spacious, with double beveled-glass doors opening onto a balcony and the sunlit courtyard below.

Being by her nature highly creative, Priscilla compensated for the dull pain of her outer world by pouring her energy into artistic expression. The inner realms of symbols, images and emotions were her domain of comfort and choice. That is where she felt truly at home, beyond the reach of judgment and scrutiny by those who found her lacking.

As she grew and matured, her painting and sculpture became more and more refined. She was becoming a deeply passionate and highly talented artist. Not surprisingly, however, she showed her work to no one for many years.

Priscilla learned to live in a secret and fascinating world of her own making, and was capable of spending hours in the magical realms of shadows and symbolism. Although this inner world provided some degree of solace for her, it never fully compensated for what she had lost or never received in the outer world.

All of Priscilla's attempts to present herself to her parents met with empty acknowledgment, at best. Finally she stopped trying, and kept herself concealed as much as possible. Her isolation and dejection were no better for her than Chrysalis' favoritism and special treatment were for him.

Though good people at heart, Samuel and Roberta were blinded by their own biases, and could not see the light of their daughter's creative spirit through the shadows they had projected onto her. They unconsciously expected less of her than of her brother, and they could not see nor would they accept any evidence that would lead them to question their perceptions.

"I don't know how she can stay down there for hours on end. It's not natural. What could she be doing?" Roberta seemed concerned as she spoke, though not alarmed. She was distractedly going about the process of mending Chrysalis' winter longstockings, while her husband relaxed with a steaming mug of tea.

"You worry too much. It's just the way she is. She knows she doesn't have much to offer, so she stays to herself. It is probably best that way." Samuel scowled slightly, then changed the subject. "What are you preparing for dinner? I have a strong hunger!"

Roberta said no more about her daughter Priscilla, yet continued to wonder about the girl's behavior. She would never think of questioning or contradicting her husband, but she was certainly free to think whatever she chose.

When the family (without Chrysalis) made its ritual sojourn into the dungeons and lower regions of the castle to attend to the wounded, frightened and imprisoned ones, Priscilla was always eager to go along. Roberta and Samuel went through the motions, not the emotions, of the ceremonial journey. They conducted these rituals as a part of what they had learned was the right thing to do, missing the deeper meaning of the practice and how it applied to what was happening in their very own family.

Priscilla felt a close kinship with all of the lost souls living below, and sometimes even chose to stay behind when it was time for her family to return to their quarters.

The warriors, beasts and children in the tunnels, caves and labyrinths seemed to recognize the neglected girl child as one of them, and she felt very at home in their presence.

♥ Priscilla's Vision

Once, while sitting alone quietly with some of the children, something strange and wonderful happened to Priscilla.

Roberta and Samuel had left about an hour earlier, and Priscilla was relaxing in the comfort of the one place where she truly fit in. In the quiet solitude that was so familiar to her, she soon became drowsy and leaned against the stone wall behind her to rest her eyes.

While drifting in a dreamy half-sleep, she was brought back to consciousness by a flicker of light. Though she couldn't be sure, it seemed to have come from the eyes of one of the children who was looking at her from a far corner of the dingy room. She looked more closely and tried to focus. Yes, there it was! A gleam of soft, radiant light was coming from that little girl's huge, staring eyes. As she watched, the light seemed to grow brighter, until it filled the whole room.

In only a brief moment, her surroundings had completely changed. The light from the little girl's eyes had transformed the dungeon into a bright and beautiful place. One by one, and with slow, deliberate care, the children in the dungeon each stood up and looked at Priscilla. To her amazement, they were actually smiling at her, in spite of their tragic circumstances. Slowly at first, then steadily gaining momentum, they began to dance and play around the room. It was at this point that Priscilla noticed the pillows, plants, toy tops and tambourines that had magically appeared all around her.

As if her body had a mind of its own, Priscilla also was suddenly up and moving, dancing and playing with the children. They all seemed filled with love and joy, as if it exuded from every pore of their little bodies. Seeing these sad, wounded and frightened children coming to such vibrant life in this way was somewhat overwhelming to Priscilla, and she began to weep. She had not known that such a depth of joy and love was possible.

Now it happened that our old friend Magus the magician was there with Priscilla, in his invisible form. He knew she would need some help in understanding what was taking place, and besides, he didn't want to miss such an event. Priscilla heard the wizard's comforting voice in her mind, as if he were a kindly grandfather coming to offer reassurance. "The joy and love you see are always here, just beneath the surface of the wounding and sorrow. You allowed its emergence through the quiet presence of your love and your acceptance of the children. You invited the divine child within each of these poor abandoned souls to come out and show herself, and show herself she did. What you saw and felt is your true destiny, though it will be some time before you will know it in full. Your path is clear, my child, and you are blessed. Sleep now, for it is not yet time for you to awaken to these realms."

Comforted and lulled by the wizard's words, Priscilla dozed for a short time. When she awoke, the room was as it had been before...except...was that little girl over there smiling? No, it couldn't be. She had even less to smile about than did Priscilla.

Her vision of the divine children had completely faded from her consciousness, as the heavy blanket of familiar thoughts and feelings shrouded her mind once again. Slowly, Priscilla arose and began her ascent to the outer world. The memory of the light, joy and love she had witnessed was deeply embedded in the recesses of her mind, and would emerge now only through her dreams and the imagery of her art.

Over time, Priscilla actually began to physically resemble the wounded children from the dungeons, a change her parents noticed with some degree of alarm. She began to choose black, gray and brown colors for her garments. Her eyes seemed likewise dark and deep, filled with the emotions of sorrow and pain. She had come to identify more closely with the children of the dungeons than with her own family. There were times when she thought of running away from home and living in the labyrinth where no one could ever find her. Her art was the only thing keeping her from doing just that. It somehow gave meaning and value to her life, and actually brought a glimmer of light into the darkness of her heavy heart and mind.

Pausing to stretch a moment before going on, Marguerite looked up among the leaves of the massive oak. The rays of the sun were filtering through the shadows of the leaves, creating dancing images on the ground at her feet. She reflected for a moment on how the shadows made the light even more beautiful, and how the light added depth and richness to the shadows. She thought of how desperately all of the Chrysalises and the Priscillas of the world need each other for the recognition of their true worth and beauty. As these thoughts slowly subsided in her mind, the silent anticipation of her audience gently brought her attention back to the task of her storytelling.

♥ A Parting of Ways

It will come as no great surprise that Priscilla and her brother did not get along too well. It was hard to tell which was fiercest, Chrysalis' hostile disdain for his sister's perceived inferiority or her angry resentment of his undeserved supremacy.

Both resented the shadow and light they had lost to the other. A typical encounter could be heard one afternoon outside Chrysalis' chamber doors. "I need the light for my painting. I cannot see the more subtle colors by the candles in my room. Just let me sit by your balcony doors for a while, it is too cold to go outside." Priscilla's pleading voice hardly concealed the contempt that she held for her brother.

The young artist had been trying to create more delicate effects in her painting ever since her experience with the children in the dungeons. She had grown tired of the heavy, bold, angry designs that were the norm in her renderings. It seemed to her that Chrysalis' room was the only place in the family's quarters that provided the amount of light she needed. For some reason that she could not quite explain, she particularly desired the light in her brother's room.

Chrysalis made no attempt to conceal his feelings in his reply. "Your stupid scratchings hold no value for anyone. Why should I let you into my chambers when I know you would only spill your ugly paint on my beautiful white rug? Go away, now. You're bothering me." Saying this, the haughty boy tossed his head and snorted as if he were too good to even talk to his lowly sister.

Struggling to contain her rage, and knowing it was useless to argue, Priscilla glared darkly at him for a moment. Then, partly in an effort to control herself and partly just to escape, she wheeled around and left without a word. She silently cursed herself for being so naive as to think that her self-centered brother might show some generosity with her. Seeking vengeance in her mind, she imagined smearing her paint all over his handsome face, his expensive garments and his precious white rug. Suddenly, she decided that she would do just that, but in a way that would cost her nothing and provide great satisfaction.

As she hurried through the hallways to her room, Priscilla could already see the images in her mind's eye. She was going to paint a large rendering on canvas of her brother standing in his chambers, he and his entire room smeared in wild, powerful strokes of her deepest and darkest pigments. First she would create the pristine cleanliness of his untarnished visage and abode. Then she would bring the darkness and color of her pain and anger to the image, smearing his misplaced light with the shadow of her dark feelings.

This painting would be for her eyes only. A sensation of surging power grew within her as her chamber door clanged shut, secluding her once again in the world only she could enter.

As he watched his sister walk away, Chrysalis was surprised to find a feeling of sadness welling up from inside him. Almost desperately, he was wishing Priscilla had stayed and fought a little longer. He could only connect with her through conflict, though he did not know why. It had always been that way. He secretly wished they could be closer, and felt somewhat ashamed of his treatment of her. He was lonely, and yet he could not tell a soul about his pain.

Deep inside, in a place he would never acknowledge even to himself, Chrysalis struggled with his own pain and darkness. However he tried to deny it or project it onto others, it never really went away. He did not like the boy who had stood there being mean to his only sister and telling her to go away. He did not like the feelings of sadness and vulnerability that came up as she disappeared down the hallway.

Chrysalis had no idea where to find the humility he would need in order to offer any concessions to Priscilla, however he might secretly care for her. He found himself moving into the familiar feeling of anger at her for causing him to have these feelings of helplessness. The anger felt much better to him. At least it gave him some sense of power over the situation. He was still far from happy, however, and found himself escaping into the dream of a place and time when he would be above and beyond all of these dark and confusing realms of emotion. It so happens that this very desire for escape led Chrysalis to his first thoughts of leaving Citadel.

Moving away from home seemed to be the key to his freedom. With visions of grandeur and fame in his mind, he planned his journey for months before announcing his intentions.

His parents were shocked when he told them. "But we had such plans for you, Chrysalis! You were being considered to succeed the Lord of Citadel when you are of age. There are many here who see you as a great leader for our people."

"And yet, it is not your plans, but mine that determine my future. I feel a destiny unfolding before me and I must fulfill it." Chrysalis felt hard and cold as he spoke these words to his parents, though it was not his intention.

The sorrow and disappointment in their eyes only seemed to push him further into his desire to escape.

When at last the time came for his departure, he quickly said his goodbyes to his family and friends, leaving feelings of rejection, pain and confusion in his wake. Only Priscilla was secretly relieved to see him go.

Having procured maps leading to the surrounding settlements, Chrysalis traveled about the country for a while, looking for a suitable place to set up his home and start his business.

Nothing felt quite right for the first few months of his search. His intention was to find a fitting place in which he could teach others what he had learned about the light, and to develop wares that corresponded to his purpose. It had to be just right to fulfill his design.

Then he found it. Chrysalis' journey came to an end in the village Aldea near the castle Corazon.

Night was falling now, and the lamplighter had begun to make his rounds, igniting the torches and lanterns that were placed in the walls and corridors surrounding the courtyard. As she bade her companions good night, Marguerite had the thought that in many ways these listeners were the only family she had now. She had outlived all of her blood kin, and had never had children of her own. She felt much of the same fondness for some of the castle dwellers, however, that she had once known for her own brothers, sisters, parents and extended family.

Glad now that the day had come to a close, the wise old woman walked slowly back to her quarters in silent reverie.

Chapter Twelve: The Other Side of the Castle Walls

The wind was strong and the skies a steely gray as the small band of loyal listeners found their places along the parapet on the tower wall. Neither the weather nor the location was particularly inviting, and yet not one of the usual number of Marguerite's listeners was missing.

The crone was finding deeper pleasure in the telling of each new part of her story, particularly as she saw the changes in those of her gathering. The adults seemed somehow more comfortable with themselves, laughing easily and at times focused and intense in their emotions. The children played exuberantly in their innocence, while there were moments listening to the story when these young ones appeared wise and knowing beyond their years.

Everyone was settled into their places now, as Marguerite resumed her tale.

♥ Sebastian's Story

As a young man growing up in the castle Corazon, the warrior Sebastian had become a physically powerful man. His labors of forging metal for shield and armor and lifting stones for the castle walls insured his prowess. His body was armored with layers of muscle on his arms, legs and torso.

It had always been thus, and as a result Sebastian had never had much time to be with his friends. In occasional quiet moments alone, he longed to be free to follow his dreams and to enjoy the company of others.

Sebastian's parents loved him very deeply. They considered him to be the perfect son. Indeed he did have a heart of gold, and wanted nothing more than to give them happiness. That's why he had continued to live with them well into his adult years. Having no knowledge of his secret longings, his parents never imagined that Sebastian was anything other than content. He consistently followed their wishes, and did more work than their other two sons combined.

His internal walls worked well at keeping his secrets concealed...too well in fact.

In moments of reflection, it seemed to Sebastian that he could open his heart to the whole world and still have more to give. Powerful passions surged within him, and he knew neither source nor outlet for them. An ache grew in his massive chest, as he longed for full expression and release.

Over time, these passions began to turn to agitation. Anger often rumbled inside him when his father gave unneeded instruction on some task. Yet he showed nothing.

Sebastian's mother was very observant of subtle feelings in her sons, and she had noticed a growing tension in him of late. One day after the noon repast she turned to him, saying, "I need some supplies from the village, Sebastian. Ask your father if he can spare you, and if so take the day and relax some on your own. You look as if you could use the diversion."

Feeling a strong sense of excitement, Sebastian went immediately to find his father. Upon receiving the older man's begrudging consent, he immediately packed a small satchel and set out.

The young shield-maker had not been outside the walls of Corazon on his own since his warrior training two years earlier. As he crossed the drawbridge and his foot touched earth, he felt a surge of energy and enthusiasm welling up from inside. It surprised and confused Sebastian to find how strong were his desires to be free.

Shaking off this momentary turmoil, he quickly struck up a vigorous pace toward Aldea, unsure of exactly what he would do when he arrived.

♥ The Battle of Sebastian and Chrysalis

As Sebastian approached market center in Aldea, he remembered a conversation with Marcelus and Samantha.

"You really must go to see this Chrysalis," Marcelus had said. "He's one of the most amazing men I've ever met. I'm inclined to believe his claims about healing and freedom from turmoil."

"Yes, it's true," Samantha agreed. "I think you'll find him intriguing. He has some kind of special power—I'd like to know what you think of him."

Feeling a sense of resolve, Sebastian began inquiring as to Chrysalis' whereabouts as he gathered the supplies his mother needed.

"Oh yes, I can tell you just how to get there," the friendly shopkeeper replied to Sebastian's query. "I've been there a couple of times myself, though I'm not quite sure what to think of this so-called merchant of light. Anyway, what do I know? Just take the main thoroughfare north of town, and you'll see the old mansion at the top of the rise as you leave the village."

By the time Sebastian finished his errands it was midmorning. Acquiring some fresh scones and dried fish to curb his appetite, he headed out to the edge of town.

Approaching the old house and outbuildings, the warrior noticed a few villagers trailing into a side door to the right of what appeared to be the merchant's shop at the front entrance. He decided to browse the shop and quickly survey its wares.

Nothing particularly appealed to Sebastian in Chrysalis' place of business. Everything was bright and sparkling, designed to catch the light. No earth tones or rich colors were anywhere to be found. The rough, dark-skinned, physical man felt uncomfortable in the shop, like he would soil or break something if he were not careful. Even the framed paintings displayed on the walls had little color or shading of any kind.

The warrior felt his body dense and heavy in the presence of so much light.

"Merchant of light indeed," thought Sebastian to himself. "Too much light, for my taste." It occurred to him that some of these objects would indeed be pleasing if placed well, standing on their own against a backdrop of darkness or shadow for contrast. As his mind wandered to leaving, he looked around for the proprietor.

Just when Sebastian had decided there was no one minding the store, he noticed an old woman dozing behind the counter.

She did not open her eyes, yet seemed to somehow know when he was looking at her. She stirred slightly as his gaze fell upon her. Still without opening her eyes, she spoke. "The merchant and his followers are next door in the meeting room. You can join them if you choose."

"Why thank you, madam," Sebastian replied. The old shopkeeper did not respond beyond her monotone statement. Shaking his head in bewilderment over the strange wares and the woman's behavior, he made his way out of the shop and around to the side door.

Entering the large well-lit room, the young warrior was surprised at the feeling that washed over him. Though decorated with many of the light-catching objects and dazzling, pristine paintings from the shop next door, the atmosphere actually seemed heavy and lifeless.

Sebastian was puzzling over this as he took a seat near the entrance. He wanted to be able to leave without too much trouble if he chose to.

His attention was immediately drawn to the speaker in the front of the room. As he turned and focused, Sebastian was struck by what he saw. "Surely, this must be him" Sebastian mumbled to himself.

Chrysalis was dressed in a full-length white robe, with oversized, open sleeves that spread like wings when he opened his arms to the side. Without realizing what was happening to him, Sebastian found himself being drawn into the spell of the light merchant before him.

The merchant's eyes were surprisingly dark, in sharp contrast to the dazzling white robe and bright sparkling lights all around. Sebastian became aware of an uncomfortable feeling taking over his body. As unpleasant as it was, he decided to allow it for a moment to see what would happen.

Vaguely, through his peripheral vision, Sebastian became aware that the others in the room were likewise entranced. The intense man speaking from behind the podium seemed to be doing something to their minds. Then, slowly, the words began to register.

"You must beware. They will pull you into the darkness, if you stray from the light even for the briefest of moments. They want to steal your soul and turn you to their evil ways. They are the masters of illusion, and will convince you that their ways will profit you and make you powerful. And yet the only profit and the only power are in the light that I bring to you, and which has drawn you here tonight. The forces of darkness are growing, and we must fight them to stay in the light. Together, standing in the light, we can conquer darkness once and for all time. You are lost without the light, and I and my teachings will bring it to you, if you remain faithful."

Sebastian's dark skin began to crawl. Though he'd not heard much, the power of the message he did hear was overwhelming. It seemed almost as if the merchant's words were closing around his brain like a cold metal clamp. His heart felt heavy in his chest. It was as if something was dying inside, and the man at the front of the room was his only hope for salvation. He could feel his identity slipping away, as if there were no difference between him and the other enraptured souls around him.

Fortunately, some part of his mind was merely observing all that was taking place. He knew that he must break out of this trance now, or something awful would follow. Feeling like a creature desperate in its struggle to be free, Sebastian felt his defiant spirit wrenching itself out of the gripping effects of the merchant's spell. After what seemed a long time, the young warrior was finally able to tear his eyes away from the podium and the intensely raving man behind it.

Looking around the room, the powerful young warrior who had been trained all of his life to shield and protect others found his heart going out to the hapless villagers. He silently reached out to them with his mind, without moving a muscle or speaking a word. This somehow seemed to break the trance of a few, who turned slowly to look at him. Try as he may, he could not manage to pull the attention of the other listeners.

Suddenly, however, he realized he had also drawn the piercing gaze of Chrysalis.

The light merchant glared at Sebastian with a look of anger and disdain that took shape in his words. "I see that one of them is among us tonight. Out of the darkness to defile our light he has come. Steer clear of this one, I tell you, and do not look into his eyes. I will deal with him. The meeting is over now, and you may return to your homes. Go now, and make haste, before he works any more of his magic on your hearts and minds. Remember always the light and who brings it to you." With that Chrysalis waved his arms to the gathering, as if he were brushing them away like insects or debris.

Some small part of Sebastian wanted to run out the door behind the villagers, who were slinking away like frightened children. But something much stronger rooted him where he stood. Walking very slowly in Sebastian's direction from the front of the room, Chrysalis spoke as the last remaining participants made their way out the door.

"So, what brings you to my gathering place, stranger, and why do you doubt me so? Your petty fears and misgivings disrupted my message tonight, and I do not take kindly to anyone leading my followers astray."

Sebastian spoke from a passion that he did not know he had. It was as if all of that great love he held inside was transformed in this moment into anger toward Chrysalis for what he had been doing to the villagers. "It is you who lead them astray. You are doing to them exactly what you caution them against. You warn them against illusions and darkness as you weave a web of illusion and darkness about them. And then to seal their fate, you offer yourself as their only salvation. You do nothing to strengthen them; you only feed their fear. I will do everything in my power to shield them from this spell you cast."

"No! You're wrong!" Chrysalis' reply was loud and almost frantic. "What I do is for their own good. I have always loved the light as I love these people, and I have a great knowledge of these things. I am the only hope they have. If you stand in my way then you must be destroyed! It is I who will protect them from you!" With these words, Chrysalis leapt at Sebastian with the intent to push him toward the door. But Sebastian was as solid as the stone walls he had built all his life, and he did not budge.

Something inside Chrysalis seemed to break in that moment. It seemed that everything he had ever believed in and worked for all of his life hinged on defeating this stranger who had come to challenge him.

Since he had left Citadel, Chrysalis' life had become ever more confusing and difficult. It seemed the harder he fought for the light the more darkness surrounded him. These things terrified him, though he had voiced his fears to no one. The truth of Sebastian's words had stung him like poisoned daggers, and yet to face this truth brought into question everything he ever thought he was. His fight now was one for his own identity, and all of his primal energies were activated.

When he found he could not move the stout Sebastian, Chrysalis began to hit him with both fists about the head and shoulders. For a moment, Sebastian did nothing to defend himself or counterattack. He became the warrior behind his shield. He felt the impact of Chrysalis' vicious blows, but he did not connect with the pain.

It seemed to Sebastian that he was watching what was going on from deep inside himself, and the violence was merely someone pounding on his walls. He suddenly realized that he could not stand being trapped inside himself one moment longer. An unfamiliar rage of white-hot intensity came rushing through this powerful man's body and mind. He felt a sudden desire to crush the insane merchant until there was no breath or life left inside him. The desire for destruction was strong in Sebastian as he reached out and violently threw his arms around the flailing Chrysalis.

With little effort at all, he was able to spin the merchant around and pin his arms to his sides with a powerful, crushing hold. The urge to kill was in him only an instant, however, before something very peculiar happened. Without knowing how or why, he had become completely aware of all of the emotions Chrysalis was experiencing. He could feel the tight, rigid fear in the merchant's body as he realized his life could be snuffed out in a few brief moments. Right behind this fear, he had an abrupt sense of Chrysalis' pain and confusion over the possibility that he was doing the villagers wrong. Then Sebastian saw something else.

Chrysalis was just another lost, wounded child, trying to find his way home. But for some reason he had become so confused that he thought he himself was the way home, and the more he tried to make it true, the more of a lie it became.

The merchant was struggling for his life now, against what seemed to be arms of steel slowly tightening their hold. He was kicking, biting, screaming and thrashing about with every ounce of energy that remained in him. All of the viciousness that Chrysalis had concealed in his efforts to live in the light was now emerging full force.

Yet Sebastian's grip was unyielding, and the frantic merchant succeeded only in draining himself of all his energy. Chrysalis became more pitiful and helpless in his feeble attempts to escape.

At last, from pure exhaustion, he went limp in his opponent's arms.

♥ An Encounter with Love

As Sebastian felt the fight leaving the merchant's body, he knew he could kill him in seconds if he chose. Yet killing was not in his nature, and with his opponent yielding so, he knew he would free him.

And then something very strange began to unfold.

Sebastian felt his heart warming in his chest, as his hold on Chrysalis began to feel more like an embrace. When he felt the merchant starting to sob softly, his walls came down and the inner floodgates opened. As though with a life of its own, the love within him came flowing out in that moment.

As the seconds passed, Sebastian became aware that it was not just Chrysalis that he was holding.

A vision unfolded before him. A world seemed to open in the strength of his embrace. There before him were merchants, warriors, lords and ladies leading dark, disheveled, men and women, wounded, frightened and radiant children from the dungeons beneath Corazon. He saw beasts coming up from the labyrinthine corridors, returning to their rightful places as guardians, regal, alive and powerful once again. All was being restored to a sense of rightness that Sebastian had only known through legend and folklore.

As these images of peace and harmony unfolded, the warrior's vision faded and he was returned to awareness of his present, awkward circumstances.

And that is when Sebastian realized that Chrysalis had begun to weep in earnest. The merchant's sobs shook the two men's bodies, and Sebastian's hold on Chrysalis came more and more to resemble the loving embrace of a friend.

It was a true meeting of darkness and light. Sebastian's almost black skin contrasted with Chrysalis' pale white flesh just as the light in the warrior's heart contrasted with the darkness in the heart of the merchant.

As the moments passed and the sobbing subsided, a profound sense of relief washed over and through the two men.

Then something even more strange began to happen.

Chrysalis started laughing. At first Sebastian thought he was still crying, because the sound and feeling was so similar. But no, this was laughter, and it was contagious.

Soon both men were laughing. Sebastian relaxed his hold and they fell back on the floor, rolling around and laughing like two little boys.

The absurdity of their situation, combined with the strange and unexplained sense of connection they now felt with each other had carried them across the threshold between joy and sorrow.

They laughed at themselves, at each other, and at the paradoxes of life. They laughed with the relief that came with release. They laughed because it felt good, and they laughed for no reason at all.

As the waves of convulsive laughter finally began to subside, Chrysalis' and Sebastian's eyes met. They approached their first sober moment since the fight had begun. Both saw a look of peace in the other's eyes, tempered and colored by the knowledge that in some strange way, they were the same.

"What happened?" Chrysalis asked Sebastian; vaguely

aware of a relaxed feeling inside him unlike any he had ever known. "I don't know," Sebastian replied. "A moment ago I wanted to kill you."

"And I you," the merchant said quietly, looking down. "I've never known such rage, and hope never to again."

"Something has changed inside me," Sebastian said in a similarly subdued tone, "for now I find that I want to be your friend." He hesitated a moment, then added, "There are many things I don't like about you, but for some reason I believe that your heart is true."

Chrysalis was quiet for a moment before speaking. The two men stood up and began straightening their disheveled garments. New awareness and understanding were unfolding inside the merchant's mind at a disorienting pace, as he spoke. "I would also like to be your friend, though I have yet to learn your name."

"I am Sebastian, castle guard from Corazon." The two solemnly shook hands and strode slowly toward the open doorway.

When they were standing outside the building, Chrysalis spoke without looking at his companion, "Though you barely know me, you are the only person who seems to have seen me for who I really am. And for some reason you seem to accept me as you see me."

He was quiet a moment longer before continuing with, "Somehow I feel that I can now stop the pretense I was living. I am tired, and my old way doesn't feel right anymore. It isn't working, as you could see in tonight's meeting. I don't know what I will do or who I am to become, but I know I am ready to change my way of being in this world."

Sebastian smiled, and spoke not a word.

A sweet sense of well being floated gently among her listeners now, as Marguerite paused to consider what was to come next. Noticing the looks of contentment on the faces of all those present, she decided to let them live with these feelings for a while, and concluded her session for the day. As they gathered their belongings and slowly made their way down the stairways, the crone observed that different ones were touching each other tenderly, in a way she had not seen before. Two of the older men had their arms draped over each other's shoulders as they walked along, talking and laughing quietly. Just before they rounded the corner, the wise old woman noticed the contrasting tones of their aged, wizened skin.

Chapter Thirteen: Emerging Power

As the morning sun's rays found their way through the battlements of the tower walls, Marguerite walked slowly toward the castle keep. She had chosen the inner stronghold of the castle's royal family for the next session of her storytelling, to bring the listeners' hearts and bodies closer to her message. The crone noticed a pleasant anticipation in her breast as she moved toward this forthcoming part of her story.

Watching the approach of the first handful of arrivals, it occurred to Marguerite that there was something different about them this morning. She had noticed before that there were subtle airs emerging among the small band of men, women and children who had become her loyal companions through the storytelling. She sensed a regal quality in the bearing of the adults, as if they felt more worth and value in the essence of their inner being. Parents seemed more firm and yet gentle with their children, who had an abundance of playful energy which they could calm and focus at will when the time came for listening.

Allowing these thoughts to drift pleasantly in her mind, Marguerite found a comfortable place to sit. She chose a place toward the side of the vast throne room, which was unoccupied at the moment. When the last of her listeners' eyes were focused on her, she began.

♥ Reunion

As the four friends finished their supper, they heard a knock coming from the outer door of the meeting room. The unexpected sound brought an abrupt halt to the conversation; as if each one present sensed that something significant was about to occur. All eyes turned now to Chrysalis.

The merchant of light had invited Sebastian, Samantha and Marcelus to dine with him, as an effort to create a sense of community in his life. Since his transforming encounter with Sebastian, Chrysalis had found new life and energy in his desire to be close to other people.

With the counsel of his friends, he had made a few journeys of his own into the lower regions of his home castle Citadel, where he was beginning to form a deeper understanding of himself.

So far, this particular evening had been a pleasant one, of good food, conversation and fellowship. In spite of the convivial feelings of the gathering however, Chrysalis felt a slight anxiety as he rose to see who was at the door.

At first he did not recognize the young woman standing there alone in the darkness, even when she lifted the hood from her face and the room's light defined her features.

"Hello, Chrysalis," the woman said quietly. There was a familiar tone in her voice, as if she had known him all of his life. Recognition slowly dawned on the merchant's mind.

"Priscilla! What...how...why, it is great to see you! Come in!"

As she entered, Chrysalis found himself overcome with joy at seeing his sister after so long a time. Without thinking, he took her in his arms and hugged her warmly. The love long trapped in his heart flowed out to Priscilla of its own accord.

It almost didn't matter that she was stiff and silent in his arms.

Tears flooded Chrysalis' eyes as he released her and looked at her once again. "It is really great to see you. We have been too long apart, and I have so much to tell you."

Priscilla was speechless. She had told herself a million times that she must be crazy to go and see that worthless bigheaded brother of hers, but for some time now the urge had been so strong she was no longer able to resist. And now, to find this warm and loving welcome was almost more than she could bear. It was hard for her mind to accept that the cold, conceited brother she had known could become the man who stood before her now. As a matter of fact, she would not let herself believe it.

"What has happened to you?" Priscilla asked in a caustic tone. "Have you been drinking some new elixir, or is this a scam to make fun of me?"

Chrysalis smiled. "I know that what you see and hear bears little resemblance to the brother you have known. I was cruel to you, and full of false love for myself. I have been emptied of that haughty fullness, and something new is emerging within me. I want to show you now the love I have always felt but was too blind to even recognize. I want to offer you the respect and honor that you deserve. Please come into my home and meet my friends. Perhaps in seeing who they are, you will know my heart."

Priscilla, still cautious and cynical in her thoughts, allowed herself to be escorted through the meeting room and into the dining area of Chrysalis' quarters.

As they entered, Sebastian sensed immediately that this woman was very special to his friend. Chrysalis was beaming as he approached the group around the table. With a grand gesture, as if introducing royalty, he said, "I have the honor and privilege of presenting to you my younger sister, Priscilla." One by one, Sebastian, Marcelus and Samantha rose and warmly greeted the stunned young woman.

Removing her cape and joining them at the table, Priscilla felt as if she were in a dream. These people were genuine and true, something that was rare in her experience. Their eyes sparkled with life and energy that seemed to touch off an excitement deep in her breast. Her doubts about her brother's sincerity began to fade, as she relaxed into the friendly atmosphere of the gathering. She started to believe that somehow he had indeed been transformed, to which the character of his friends gave testimony.

When Samantha asked about her vocation, Priscilla was surprised at how easily she was able to describe her art and sculpture, as well as her dreams of future projects. The kind and sincere regard that these people held for her was like a warm cloak enveloping her on a cold night. This is what she had always wanted from her family, and had never received. As these thoughts of her painful past arose, Priscilla felt the familiar darkness return.

Sensing the shift in his sister's emotions, Chrysalis directed the focus to Marcelus and a new business venture he was starting. The conversation continued to move easily around the table, so that Priscilla was put at ease once again. The atmosphere was further warmed by the steaming bowls of venison, pork and potatoes within easy reach, complemented by ample platters of fresh fruit and vegetables and frothy mugs of ale.

As the evening progressed, Priscilla felt at moments that she had always been there, talking and laughing with these wonderful people. Soon the hour was getting late, and Marcelus and Samantha took their leave, with Sebastian close to follow.

Left alone with her brother, Priscilla felt awkward and shy. In spite of her pleasant feelings, she still held anger toward him. She tried to talk herself out of the recurring thoughts of resentment, but they would not go away. The uncomfortable silence between them was palpable.

For his part, Chrysalis wanted nothing more than to share his new awareness with his sister, yet he wisely considered that he should wait until the morning. Caught between his desire to talk and an awareness of the late hour, he said, "I have a spare room for you. I'm sure you are tired from your journey and would like to take your rest." Priscilla answered with a silent nod of her head. As he showed her to her quarters, Chrysalis was very aware of the uneasiness that was between them. He was confident, however, that they would be able to talk openly soon, and he went to sleep with a prayer in his heart that his sister would soon find the joy that he and his friends had come to know.

On the afternoon of the following day, Priscilla found it easy to allow her feelings to flow into the calm, open space that Chrysalis provided. The two siblings had spent the day catching up, deliberately keeping the subject matter light. They were sitting in the rear garden of Chrysalis' home enjoying a mild breeze in the afternoon sunlight.

With no warning, Priscilla began to feel her anger moving about in her belly like a restless animal in a cage. She knew she had to give it voice, and secretly hoped it wouldn't damage her newfound connection with her brother.

"I'm still angry with you," she said. "You have no idea what it was like for me living in your shadow all those years. And you never did a thing to change it. As a matter of fact, you loved it. My suffering was directly to your benefit." She couldn't look at him as she spoke. The only way the determined young woman could get to the bottom of these emotions was to give them her full focus without the distraction of the compassionate man her brother had become.

"You relished the attention that was showered on you by Mother and Father. You never stood up for me, spoke out for me or came to my rescue. I remember you only coming to my room a few times, and it was usually because you were angry about something, or needed something from me. Yet, like a fool, I loved you and wanted your attention all the same. How could I have been so foolish?"

Priscilla could feel the tears welling up as she spoke, but raised her voice to keep from crying. She wanted to keep her power, and didn't want her tears to diminish her. She looked at him defiantly.

"You had everything, and I lived in the basement. I guess that's why I felt so comfortable with the children in the dungeons. I was one of them! And you loved it!" The young woman paused, as something in her brother's eyes made it hard for her to focus her anger.

"You're right," Chrysalis said quietly but clearly as he looked at his sister. "I agree with everything you have said. You don't know me completely, and you don't know everything I went through. But what you have said makes sense to me, especially when I imagine how things must have been for you."

Chrysalis was not threatened by his sister's anger or her accusations. He had thought many of the same things about himself, and worse.

As much as Priscilla wanted to keep her anger strong, she found it almost completely subsiding at this point. She caught a glimpse of pain in her brother's eyes, and for the first time considered that his childhood had not been entirely without suffering.

"Someday I will tell you what it was like for me," he went on. "But for now I just want to be here with you, in a new way." After a pause, he continued with, "I'm not that kid you grew up with, but I take responsibility for any way I hurt you."

Priscilla allowed the tears to come now. Chrysalis sat quietly, not wanting to interrupt her expression.

"The worst part was that I actually hated you," Priscilla said quietly, with her eyes lowered. "I blamed you for everything that happened to me, and it wasn't all your fault. Now I just want to let all of that go. I'm tired of feeling so bitter and miserable."

"We must acknowledge that we were children, growing up in a home created by our parents. They favored me, and I had no power over that. They relegated you to the shadows, and you had no power over that. They are responsible for what they created in our home, just as you and I are now responsible for who we become as adults."

Chrysalis spoke these words in a somber tone. He was reluctant to speak in a denigrating manner toward his mother and father, yet his commitment to integrity and truth was strong.

"I have had the same thoughts," Priscilla added after a pause. "They were the ones with the freedom to change what was happening. They are responsible for what happened then, and we are responsible for how we deal with it now. I for one will not be limited by my past. I choose to love you. You are my brother—the only one I have--and I am deeply grateful for our reconciliation after all these years."

"As am I," Chrysalis responded through a smile that shone from his very full heart.

Over the hours and days of their visit, the buried love within the estranged siblings continued to emerge to fill the space so long cold and empty between them. Laughing and crying together, they swapped stories and reminisced late into each evening.

And they forgave their parents—for being human beings, and for their shortcomings as parents.

Marguerite smiled at the moist eyes among her listeners. They had felt the heart of her story, and she took a moment to allow this feeling to take root. Silently, the crone sat and breathed deeply, looking into the hearts of each of those present, one by one. The unspoken message she gave them was one of peace and reconciliation. She silently encouraged them in that moment to reach out to all who had wronged them, and to those to whom they had done wrong. The fullness of those moments spoke volumes about love, acceptance, grief and reconciliation.

♥ A Transition of Power

When she felt moved to do so, Marguerite returned to her tale. The silent exchange she had experienced with her listeners had come to completion, and the shift in their energy let her know that they were ready for her to continue.

The lord and lady of the castle Corazon had been abroad on political business as long as Marcelus could remember. Their lives were the stuff of legend for him and Samantha, who had been but babes in their mothers' arms in the year of the noble couple's departure. No one had expected that they would be away so long.

When the minstrels and bards brought news of Lord Peter and Lady Delia's adventures and escapades, it was clear that neither business nor politics had kept them away. The poems and songs told of their encounters with sea monsters, pirates and evil warlords, in which the couple had many close calls and narrow escapes. They had apparently been on some kind of quest, seeking adventure for its own sake and avoiding the mundane responsibilities that were theirs in Corazon.

No one knew how much to believe, of course, as the bards and minstrels were known to take much poetic license in the telling of their tales.

The citizens of Corazon had fared well despite the absence of the noble family to provide them leadership and guidance. There had been no talk of replacement for their lordships, as everyone fully expected that they would return one day.

Then the news came...this time from a royal messenger on horseback rather than a bard.

It was rare that news arrived in such a manner in Corazon. This message was official, and the horseman was attired in the garb of nobility, indicating service to a high court in a neighboring region. Word of his arrival spread rapidly throughout the castle as he rode slowly to the center courtyard, children and dogs at his heels. Soon a fairly large gathering had convened to hear him.

Unfurling his scroll and holding it open with both hands, he read, "His Royal Highness Prince Phillip regrets to inform you that he has it on good authority that your own Lord Peter and Lady Delia have perished at sea. He offers his condolences, and his assistance if any be needed. You may choose among yourselves for new leadership, subject to your magistrate's approval. You will be expected to pay your taxes on time as always."

The messenger looked briefly at the small gathering of merchants and community leaders that were gathered, re-rolled his scroll and placed it back in his pouch. As he got back on his horse and rode away, the group remained still and silent, stunned by what they had heard.

Over the following weeks, more news trickled in via travelers and itinerant merchants. It was told that the unfortunate lord and lady of Corazon had gone down with their ship in a violent storm, on their final voyage home.

Peter and Delia had apparently fought the storm long and hard, under the guidance and leadership of their able ship's captain. But alas, their efforts had been to no avail. Some local fishermen found the ship's wreckage washed ashore on the morning following the storm, with one survivor. The ship's boatswain, barely alive himself, told of the noble couple's valiant attempts to survive.

Although it had been many years since their departure from the castle, the occasional reports and constant expectations of their return had made it seem as if the Lady Delia and her husband Lord Peter had been gone only a short while. They had somehow lived on in Corazon, larger than life in the hearts and minds of the castle dwellers through the oft-told tales of their adventures.

Their flaws of haughtiness and judgment had faded over time, the illusion of their greatness being unchallenged by their actual presence.

In the weeks and months following the news of the Lord and Lady's untimely death, something changed in Corazon. It was as if a spirit of hope and inspiration had departed, and a cloud of despair made its way into the hearts of the castle dwellers.

There was much talk of seeking new leaders for the people. This first came to Samantha's attention when she overheard a conversation between a villager and one of the castle guards. It was late one afternoon just before sundown, and the two were at table outside the castle brewery, talking over mugs of ale.

"They tell me he's spending a lot of time in Corazon now, with that merchant Marcelus and his friends, of whom our own

Sebastian is one. They pass long hours together." It was the castle guard who spoke, with his head lowered somewhat as though he did not want to be heard. "Chrysalis has changed quite a bit since the early days of his ravings about the light in the village. His associations with the warriors Sebastian and Samantha have been good for him. He seems more down to earth now."

At the mention of her name, Samantha turned away from where the two were sitting, not wanting to be recognized until she was able to learn more of what was going on. Her table was several cubits from theirs, and they had not noticed her as yet. She pulled the hood to her cloak a little farther over her head.

The villager spoke next. "In my mind, he has all of the qualities we need in a leader. He has a radiance of royalty about him that gives the impression that he is blessed. He is inspiring, noble in his bearing, and seems to be gaining wisdom and humility over time. Let's talk with the others and see how best to approach him with our proposition."

With that the two men parted ways. The guard returned to his duties, and the villager made his way home through the castle gates. Keeping her head lowered, Samantha waited until they were out of sight before she rose and returned to her quarters to think over what she had heard.

Before falling asleep that night, Samantha made up her mind to say nothing of this to Chrysalis or anyone else. It was not her way to spread rumors when she had so little information. She was quite curious, however, as to what might happen next.

Her questions were answered only a few days later when she and her friends were casually discussing some castle business in the main courtyard. A large crowd was approaching from the main entrance, and among them were the villager and the guard that Samantha had overheard outside the castle brewery.

The leader of the group was carrying the castle banner, an elegant flag with brilliant colors bearing the insignia of Corazon. Such pomp was only used to signify the presence of royalty and nobility, and at first the group of friends were confused by its unexpected appearance.

It was the leader of the group that carried the banner, and he that addressed the group now in a very formal manner. "My name is Aurelius, and I was attendant to Lord Peter when his presence still graced us here in the castle Corazon. I speak now for my companions who have gathered with me today." The man paused, shuffled his feet and seemed to be gathering himself for what he was about to say.

♥ An Offer to Chrysalis

"We have observed your stature and wisdom over the past year, Lord Chrysalis. After much deliberation, we have chosen you as the one to provide us with the inspiration and leadership we need in Corazon. Since receiving the news of the deaths of Lord Peter and Lady Delia, we have been without a focus for our homage. We believe that you can serve us well in such a role. We are a simple people, and need leaders in order to feel right with things. Of course, we have our magistrate, but he is shouldering too much of late. Being the only one with authority in matters of law, he finds the burden is telling on him.

Though he was not visible to those present, the wizard Magus now stood behind Chrysalis, his hands on the shoulders of the merchant of light. This was a moment the wizard had anticipated, and he was determined to have his input into the momentous decision-making at hand. As he looked into the hearts and souls of Chrysalis, Samantha, Marcelus, Sebastian and Priscilla, however, the wise old man could see that he had no real cause for concern. Shadowy images of many familiar visages moved within and among this group of emerging sovereigns, as they turned to speak to each other with their eyes.

Magus saw the spirits of ancient kings and queens moving like wisps of white clouds among his beloved students and companions. He sensed the presence of Marion of the Temple Serenus, the divine Serai, and the primitive power of the lions Regalis and Leone. The wizard knew that the wisdom and equanimity of these evolved souls were available to the group of five before him. It was from this wisdom that Chrysalis now spoke, having received the confirmation he needed from the eyes of his virtuous friends.

"Thank you, my brothers and sisters, for the honor you would bestow upon me. I am deeply touched by your desire that I provide you with the inspiration you need in this time of loss and disorientation. I answer you now with a mixture of regret and joy. I regret that I cannot give you the nourishment of hope and inspiration you ask of me. It is with ecstatic joy, peace and serenity that I tell you that what you want is already yours. What you admire in me is but a reflection of what you would become, and it is to that becoming that I commit myself and my energies.

"My companions and I will work together to show you the way to that which you seek. Each of us here, my sister Priscilla the artist, the merchant Marcelus, and the warriors Samantha and Sebastian offer you friendship, counsel and the inspired vision we have attained through contact with our divine essence, a birthright we all share. Our individual journeys have led us through the darkness of our hearts and minds, where we have found the light of healing, wisdom, and the sovereign presence that draws you to us today. We ask only that you return, as we have, to the story of the divine child for your guidance and teaching. In the dungeons of Corazon, you will find the wounded, lost, frightened and frightening, waiting for your acknowledgment and embrace. As you open your hearts and minds to these abandoned and rejected ones, the divine child will emerge to greet you, warming your body and soul with her love.

"At no time will we allow you to project your light onto us, asking that we be what you have not yet become. To do so would harm us all. We are not above you, and will accept no power or privilege other than that which we have attained through our own true and honest effort.

"Our vision for you is the same as for us. We would but see the emergence of divine sovereignty in everyone we meet, as we work to facilitate the constant birth of this new life and energy in each one of ourselves. This will come only through your courage, wisdom and humility, qualities that grow from within, as you turn to face the vast depths of who you are.

"We will tell you our stories, and as you listen, you will hear your own. We are all connected through our stories, and through the story of the divine child. We are each on a solitary path, and yet we are not alone. We are all a part of the same story, though none can play your part but you. Corazon will have no single noble family, because together we will all be a noble family. Each of us will lead and follow in our own way, according to our individual experience and need. Life will be much easier and far more challenging than you have ever imagined. This is my response to your request. We offer you nothing, and we offer you everything."

The crowd of villagers and castle dwellers were spellbound. As Chrysalis was speaking, his words seemed to be coming from his companions as well as from him. Their deep and compassionate eyes were focused intently on their audience. This event and Chrysalis' words became a thing of legend over time. As the stories of the encounter were later told and retold, some accounts had it that Samantha was the one who spoke, while others said it was Marcelus, Sebastian, or Priscilla. And, though they were doubted by many, two of the older women in the crowd swore that they saw the wizard Magus standing behind Chrysalis, and that it was he who did most of the talking.

The crackling energy of magic was in the air about the heads of Marguerite and those of the gathering in the castle keep of Corazon. The crone felt moved to speak directly to her listeners, although briefly. "Let the life of the story live in you for a while, unmolested by your thoughts and conversation. A wizard lives in each of you, and would have his way with this moment." Recognizing the unspoken signal for a break, the listeners stood, stretched and wandered off, staying to themselves in honor of what they were experiencing at the guidance of the wise Marguerite.

Chapter Fourteen: The Telling of the Stories

The saga resumed when less than an hour had passed Eagerness and anticipation were building in Marguerite and her listeners, as the story's momentum gathered and grew.

Although most of the villagers and castle dwellers still wanted an individual sovereign to whom they could turn for inspiration and leadership, they found themselves increasingly intrigued by the stories and the unique form of leadership provided by the five companions. The tales of their adventures into dark realms and the amazing discoveries they made there were fascinating to all who chose to listen.

When Samantha spoke of her struggles with her sword and the powerful aggressive energy that erupted within her, her audience was always spellbound. Her kind, radiant persona provided such striking contrast to her description of the dark warrior in the labyrinth that the minds of her listeners were expanded through the mere effort of understanding. Blending the gentle grace of love and compassion with the sharp, piercing energy of the warrior's spirit, Samantha provided an image of wholeness, peace and power that was completely new and inspiring for all those fortunate enough to be near and hear her.

The powerful woman warrior was speaking now to a group of girls and young women who had gathered to admire her proficiency with the sword. She was training younger warriors in an open field designated for such activities, in the south corner of the castle grounds.

Samantha took a break from the training, and sat among those who had come to watch. "What you see in me is but a reflection of who you are and who you are to become. And yet, you will be your own person, different from me as I am from those who were my mentors.

I wish to tell you now about something that you may know little of. In my journeys to the dungeons, I did not always return alone. There truly are wounded and frightened children down there. Waifs, urchins, lost and confused souls hide in those shadows. It is our responsibility to bring them out into the light, for our own benefit as much as for theirs.

"As I have brought these precious ones from the shadows into the light, my power has grown beyond what I had imagined possible. I have learned through this process that true power resides in vulnerability, and weakness only comes from fragmentation and denial of who we are. My clarity, focus and vigilance as a warrior are enhanced by my sensitivity to my wounds and fears. I no longer pretend to be anything other than I am, and the sphere of safety around me grows. As a warrior, it is my mission to expand the field of peace and security that is needed for the safe emergence of the precious children."

One of the girls in the small crowd watching Samantha seemed momentarily transfixed as she stared unfocused in the direction of the woman warrior.

The child Murial was known for her visions, and one was capturing her attention now. In place of the everyday warrior garb of leather jerkin, tunic and trousers, the gifted girl saw Samantha adorned in glowing white robes and a golden crown perfectly suited to her beauty and bearing.

And then the child's private image shifted and deepened.

As sparkling mists passing over the bright face of a waterfall in sunlight, Murial's vision now revealed the regal beauty and wisdom of a queen shimmering and glistening in Samantha's countenance. A quiet and graceful sovereignty was reflected in all of her features. At the same time, the penetrating focus and sharp clarity of the warrior-spirit was evident in each of her movements and subtle gestures.

As quickly as it had come, the image faded, and the child saw Samantha in her normal attire once again. Such "spells," as adults around her called them, often took the gifted Murial. She herself was accustomed to their coming and going, and no longer questioned them.

Murial had caught a glimpse of Samantha's spiritual and sovereign essence, as revealed in the labyrinthine realms. The child's gift of vision took her past the world of temporary appearances into a realm where she could discern the true nature of a transformed and transforming Samantha.

Somehow sensing what had occurred, the warrior glanced at the girl sitting before her at the front of the small group. As the child came out of her trance, she saw the woman she adored smiling at her, and responded in kind. Both hearts were filled in this moment, and no words were spoken as the group slowly dispersed and each went her separate way.

Satisfied that she had connected with the hearts and minds of her listeners, the old storyteller leaned back and relaxed into silence before continuing. She smiled at the spark of delight awakening in the eyes of her listeners.

As Marguerite gazed briefly at the mosaics etched into the ceiling and walls of the castle keep, she thought of Chrysalis. There were pieces of his story that needed telling, and they fit nicely at this particular point of transition.

♥ Chrysalis Tells His Story

On a crisp autumn morning, the merchant of light was in his usual place of prayer and meditation, in the east tower of Corazon overlooking the forest that led to Aldea. While retaining his home near the village, Chrysalis was spending more time in the castle of late. He felt a need for the sense of community that was there, and enjoyed the ethereal solitude of the high towers on the castle walls.

The merchant was unaware of Aurelius as he approached cautiously with his friends. Though not wanting to disturb Chrysalis' solitude, they were desperate in their curiosity as to what gave this unusual man his powers. Each one of those approaching had ambitions, believing that they could learn from this inspired merchant who had apparently attained a level of greatness they sought.

Not surprisingly, these villagers and castle dwellers that were drawn to Chrysalis and his special gifts were exactly the ones who needed to hear his story.

Stirring from his deep stillness, Chrysalis felt a presence and turned slowly toward Aurelius and his companions. "A bright good morning to you my friends. Come and join me. Let us bring in this new day in spirited conversation." The immediate warmth of his greeting created a feeling of grateful humility in the small group of men and women. They gathered quietly around Chrysalis, not really knowing what to say next.

It was Aurelius who first found his voice.

"Speak to us of how you came to be who you are, and from whence comes your serenity."

Chrysalis could see the sincere desire in Aurelius' heart. Looking away across the parapet to some distant point on the horizon, he began by recounting his experiences as a boy in Citadel. His voice held a deep resonance, reflecting the passion and power in what he was saying.

"I was a favored child. My parents held me in the highest of esteem, always expecting and believing the best of me. They provided nothing for me in learning the grace and value of humility. I had everything I wanted, and learned to believe that I was entitled to this privilege.

"Without deciding to, I began to think of myself as superior. That was how my parents saw me, and I learned who I was through their eyes and through their treatment of me."

Looking from time to time into the eyes of his listeners, Chrysalis could see fleeting images of himself reflected in their visages. Clearly, some of them had been favored in their own families.

"But I was not a happy boy. Something inside me did not feel right. I didn't understand it at the time, but I somehow knew that I was not the perfect being they saw in me. I had my fears, doubts and confusion, and yet could speak no word of these. I felt that the love of my parents depended on my fulfillment of their image of me. So I hid my shortcomings and self-doubt, and grew ashamed of this secret world inside me.

"Over time I grew angry. I was angry at the inferiority of those I saw as beneath me, and angry at the inferiority I sensed in myself. Most of the time, I took this anger out on my sister, and occasionally my mother. It seemed to me that of all people, women were the most inferior, and worthy of belittlement.

"I was not to learn how wrong I was for many years."

As they journeyed together in Chrysalis' story, the small gathering shared the pain and confusion of his time of deluded greatness as the merchant of light in Aldea. They felt his grief and relief as he recounted his desperate struggle with Sebastian at the end of his time of growing torment.

"You see, the shadow I buried arose to consume me," Chrysalis said in summary to this part of his story. "I knew nothing of it, so I recognized it not as it spoke to my mind and heart, telling dark stories of fear, power and tyranny. I had learned in my childhood that I was so blessed that I indeed had no darkness within me, and that had become my belief.

"Sebastian saw through my veil of confusion, and helped me come to terms with who I really am.

"And now I have learned that within my shadow is something I cannot live without. Since journeying to its depths and retrieving the treasures hidden there, I have known more joy, love and passion for life than I ever imagined possible. I will tell you now of my journey into my own darkness, and of what I found there.

"It was my encounter with Sebastian that first showed me how light can be found in the heart of darkness. All of the rancor I had denied in myself came out of me in that moment when I wanted more than anything to take his life. The force and power within me shocked, thrilled and horrified me to the depths of my being.

"I will be eternally grateful for the love and strength within my warrior-friend Sebastian that would not allow me to kill him, nor him to kill me. The loving embrace with which he surrounded my dark desire to destroy allowed something precious and wonderful to emerge from deep within me. I was overwhelmed with a feeling of grace within seconds of wanting to kill. Just beyond that which I most feared was that which I most desired.

"In the days and weeks that followed, prior to the arrival of my sister Priscilla, I faced and struggled with the many and diverse elements of my soul I had so long sought to deny. During long, sleepless nights I fell headlong into the dungeons of my soul. There I found pain, turmoil, fear, hatred and confusion that seemed they would devour me and take me into eternal suffering. And yet it was through the gates of this very personal hell that I found insight, healing and peace beyond anything I had known in the heights of my false glory and perceived greatness.

"On one particular night, I made a journey into the dungeons of Citadel, the castle of my birth. I had been guided and advised by my friends Marcelus and Samantha, and felt somewhat prepared for the path before me. As this path I was to follow rested in my very soul, I was able to travel without leaving my quarters in the village.

"By this time, Samantha had introduced me to Magus the magician, who was known to have powers that are helpful on inner journeys. He was with me as I descended that night, though I could not see him clearly. While his presence brought some comfort, at the moment of entering the darkness of the lower regions I felt totally alone and afraid.

"Still and cold as a statue, I stood frozen at the entrance to the labyrinth, thwarted before my journey had begun. My thoughts were racing and colliding with each other in complete chaos.

"Then a still, quiet voice slowly made itself known to me from deep in the recesses of my mind. It seemed so far away I couldn't tell if it was in my head or outside. The words gradually became clear.

"'There is light here as well, within the depths of the darkness. Your fear would tell you that you are alone, and there is only danger ahead. Know that you are guided, guarded and gifted on your journey, and your knowing of this makes it so.'

"I knew it was Magus' voice, and the mere sound of it reassured me, though the meaning of his words hovered almost beyond my mind's reach.

"As my understanding of the wizard's message grew, I suddenly found myself in a completely different location. I looked around and blinked, realizing gradually that I was deep within the labyrinth. As I recovered from shock at the unexpected change, my vision slowly focused on the dark tunnel entrances that wound and twisted away from me in all directions, leading off into the labyrinthine maze.

"I caught a movement just then, over my left shoulder. It was the fleeting image of my sister Priscilla. It occurred to me then that she had traveled this way many times before me, and the thought of her somehow brought me comfort.

"That momentary ease was quickly interrupted by something very strange and unnerving, however. What appeared to be a ribbon of darkness, a deeper black even than its surrounds, pulled at my midsection from one of the tunnel openings. Despite my fear, I moved in response to this urging, stooping low to enter the passageway.

"After feeling my way in absolute darkness for what seemed to be hours, I became aware of a faint glow some distance ahead. The light flickered, and then disappeared for moments at a time.

"And suddenly I arrived at its source.
"I found myself in a larger space, the rock ceiling above me a good fifteen feet high. In the dim light, the walls eluded the reach of my vision.

♥ The Frozen Child

"As my eyes adjusted to the strange yellowish light, a slight movement caught my attention. The image of a small boy slowly clarified before me. He was sitting very still, huddled against a wall in the shadows. Carefully, I moved closer until I began to make out the features of his face.

"When I could focus enough to see his eyes, a sudden chill ran through me. His hollow, empty gaze drew me in, as if it were magnetic, or a vacuum. He must have been in some kind of trance, completely unaware of my presence.

"Without knowing why, I sat down on the cold stone floor of the cave-like room. I had a strong urge just to be with this boy. As my body relaxed and my mind cleared, a strong affinity for the child grew within me. It slowly dawned on me that he was part of my self, always felt and never faced.

"Then, I was aware of a powerful and unexpected desire to run away. For a moment it took all of my energy just to stay put. Thankfully, the fear passed almost as suddenly as it had come.

"Gradually, I moved closer to the boy. When I had progressed only inches in his direction, I noticed his eyes growing wider in fear. He was aware of my presence now, but didn't seem to know me. I knew that I must earn his trust.

"I decided to let him take the lead in any interaction that might follow.

"As I sat there breathing deeply and trying to create a safe presence for this little one, the sight of him slowly brought me growing insight into my own life.

"In my special, privileged status at Citadel, I had never known, honored or acknowledged the lonely, frightened child within me. And at times the feelings nearly consumed me, though they remained deep within my unconscious realms.

"And now, for the first time, I was discovering something valuable beyond measure in these depths.

"Knowing it would be a long time before this child would accept my love, I simply held his huddled image in my heart. I kept the entire picture intact, the child and my adult self in the underground chamber, with me waiting patiently at a safe distance. I returned to this image many times in the following weeks before I began to notice a change in the boy's countenance.

"Gradually, his fear began to subside, and he slowly moved those huge frightened eyes to focus in my direction. I felt an unspoken invitation in his expression to move closer, and I did.

"Eventually I was able to touch him, and even hold him in my arms.

"As I held him that first time, I was almost overwhelmed with the trembling waves of fear and sorrow that washed from his body into mine. Yet I was able to hold a loving presence through this, and I could feel his trembling dissolve slowly into calm.

"As I literally wrapped my adult body around his tiny frame, I realized we were in the exact same posture. In my attempt to cradle him and provide total protection and love, my body had assumed the exact same position that he was in. My feeling was one of loving protection and nurturing and his was one of fear, yet we were very much the same.

"And now this child and I wept the same tears, together. He was the child I had once been and still was, deep in my heart. And I the adult was there, powerfully connected with this vulnerable part of my soul for the first time.

"And then it was time to bring him home. No longer lost, alone and unacknowledged, he belonged with me. I wanted him with me. With him nestled snug and secure in my arms, I slowly made my way through the winding tunnels toward the light of day.

"As we emerged from the shadows and the daylight illumined the child's tiny frame, I was able to see him clearly for the first time. His skin was lifeless, and his body frail. He struggled to hide in the folds of my shirt, as if the light frightened him.

"Then I knew. He did not belong in the light of day. This boy belonged inside, tucked away safe and sound in a place of nurturing and love. With these thoughts, I felt him move into my inner self, coming to a resting place in my heart. He needed healing and care, and I created the perfect place for him there inside me. I was the only protection he had, and I was fiercely committed to his care and well being.

"As I tended to the little one over the ensuing days, weeks and months, I knew more profoundly than ever that he represented what I had denied in myself, and embracing him was essential to my becoming whole. I had unwittingly projected him onto those around me, trying helplessly to heal myself by saving the world from suffering. This had brought only unhappiness for me and for all those I tried to help.

"As this child grew to trust me, I felt his little body relaxing, healing and becoming strong. My breathing slowed and deepened as this occurred, and I felt a new power emerging within my body.

"You see, my friends, holding this child frozen within me all those years had drained tremendous energy from my body and mind. This precious energy was returning to me now, as the child was returned to his rightful place and given the honor and care that were rightfully his."

Pausing for a moment to stretch and yawn, Chrysalis looked at Aurelius and his friends. He was struck by the intensity and depth of their focus. As he had hoped, some of them had made the journey with him, and were applying the story to their own lives.

Marguerite, like Chrysalis, broke from the storytelling. Looking about the castle keep for a corner to nestle into, she quietly rose and walked away. The gathering dispersed, though they stayed within view of the crone so as to know the moment of her return. A sense of urgency was strong in the listeners as the story grew in power and depth. Each knew that there was something to gain from every element of the tale, and they did not want to miss a single morsel of this goodness.

As Marguerite relaxed during the break time and settled into a restful state, a vision of Priscilla as a child appeared before her. As she watched, the girl looked into her eyes, imploring her to see and understand something of great import. Priscilla turned away, and seemed to slowly transform within the field of the old woman's inner vision. She seemed to be in a trance, staring adoringly at two people in front of her. They were her parents. She was fixated on her mother and father, looking at them as if they were godlike and perfect in her mind. Marguerite suddenly knew where her story needed to go next. After a few more moments of rest, she returned to the waiting group of listeners. When they were quiet and their attention was hers, she began speaking.

♥ Priscilla Shares Her Story

In what had become a customary gathering, Chrysalis and his group of friends convened in the courtyard for conversation and libation. Everyone was there except Priscilla.

Chrysalis found himself surprisingly ill at ease. These feelings subsided the moment he saw his sister emerge from a fabric shop across the way. He called to her and invited her to join them.

"Priscilla, will you share your journey with our friends?" By now, the small group was growing, and there were over a dozen in the gathering. Priscilla was quiet for a moment.

"I would be honored," she said quietly, choosing a place to sit near her brother. The young artist's manner and dress drew a certain intrigue from the group of listeners. She was different from the others, quieter and more mysterious in her dark hooded cloak and humble posture.

Priscilla straightened her back and let her hood fall around her shoulders. Her dark hair framed her alabaster skin to provide a hauntingly beautiful contrast of shadow and light. The intense young artist looked slowly around the group and began to speak.

"I will tell of a part of my journey which for me was perhaps the most daunting. It was the point of my deepest darkness, providing entry to the greatest light.

"I had made many journeys into the dungeons of Citadel by the time of this story, and was quite comfortable with the lower realms. Something was not quite right, however.

"In spite of the relief and joy I experienced bringing the wounded and frightened children up from the darkness, I was still at times drawn into a deep despair. Thoughts of ending my life would burst into my mind with no warning or understanding on my part. That's when I knew there was work yet to be done. I began planning another visit to the lower regions.

"The way into the dungeons was familiar to me by now, but on this particular journey I went deeper, and was drawn into new directions. Suddenly I found myself in a part of the labyrinth that I had never seen before.

"A deep rumble within the walls gradually made its way into my awareness, signaling the presence of a protector spirit. I had learned by now to move straight into these places, holding love in my heart and remembering that all protection originates from love.

"The armored warrior that appeared before me seemed familiar, and it appeared to recognize me as well. I had encountered this same protector on other journeys, and befriended it many times. Such alliances are not always steady, however, and must often be renewed — especially when entering new territory.

"Standing tall and stalwart, the menacing being moved between me and the small doorway now shielded in its shadow. In a voice that was more growl than speech, it said, 'It is your fault! You are the cause of all the suffering. You brought the pain upon yourself, and you deserved it! You should have never turned away from those who provided for you. You have no right to enter here and disturb this place!'

"Knowing from earlier experience that it was pointless to argue with the protectors, I thanked her for revealing herself, and for the strength of her protection.

"'I am grateful for your guarding of this sacred place. You have served for many years now, and your job is well done. You are a part of me, and I accept you. Your power is mine. You serve me, I do not serve you.'

"She relaxed her rigidity ever so slightly at my words.

"At that point, I simply moved toward the warrior with open arms and heart. With no doubt in my actions, I embraced this powerful being, silently thanking her once again for her efforts to protect me.

"Although I had done this before on numerous occasions, it always surprised me to find the warrior shrinking in my embrace. As I pulled it into myself, its energy moved into my muscles and I felt a renewed strength and sense of power. I knew this strength would be useful to me in completing the task that lay ahead.

"I pushed the small door open and stooped to enter. A pale and sickly light followed the door's shadow across my garments. Quickly my attention was taken by the sound of a child's voice chattering away in a frantic manner. The combined effect of the pale light and the ingenuine sound of the child's voice brought a sense of dread that shuddered through me as I straightened up and looked cautiously around the room.

"As my vision adjusted to the strange light, I was surprised to find not one but three beings before me, only a few feet away. There was the little girl who had been making all the noise. She appeared to be around three or four years of age, and was jumping around erratically between two adult figures. I recognized the child as a younger version of myself, and the adult figures were thin, two-dimensional representations of my parents. The child was holding the parents' hands. The adults appeared like as thin scroll-like replicas of themselves, with empty smiles on their faces. They were totally still and lifeless. They were not real.

"Here she was, the part of myself that had always lived in illusions of happiness, pretending that everything was wonderful when it was not. The caricatures of my parents showed the frail reality of her illusion. The loud noises the little girl was making were to drown out the voices of truth, which would, if allowed, quietly tell the stories of rejection and neglect which had by now become familiar to me.

"Although I had examined and healed many of my wounds, this child remained caught in her illusion. I felt sad when I looked at her. I realized that her picture of reality had been necessary for a time in my past, although it had clearly outlived its usefulness at this point. She herself was a protector of sorts, working frantically to maintain an illusion that hid a painful reality.

"The voice of Magus in my mind spoke now. 'Go and be near this child, so that she may choose you, when she is ready. You are real, and you are truly here. These frail imitations of parents offer her nothing. She will come to you, in time, if you are patient and hold a loving presence.'

"I could see that the little girl was tired. It took a lot of energy to pretend that a very sad situation was happy. Sensing how close I could come to the child without disturbing her, I moved forward slowly and sat down. When I thought she might be able to hear me, I said simply, 'I am here. It's okay. You don't have to change. Thank you for trying so hard to keep everything happy.

I know you're tired, and maybe a little scared. It's all right. I'll take care of you. I'll never leave you. I am here for you, when you are ready. You can stay with them as long as you like. I love you exactly as you are.'

"At first my presence seemed to frighten her, and she chattered even more loudly. Then, as I repeated the same words over and over and waited patiently, she gradually started quieting down and looking my way more often.

"'Now hold that image in your heart,' the quiet voice spoke inside my mind. `Do not leave or move away until the child is in your arms of her own accord, and feels the warmth of your presence. Then you can fully know the truth, and understand your own innocent nature.'

"I followed this guidance for months before the hapless little girl finally sank exhausted into my arms and wept. Feeling the truth of my love allowed her to know the emptiness of her past. The thin, artificial images of my parents quickly faded as she relaxed with me. We wept tears of joy and sorrow together, for her sorrow and healing were mine as well."

Feeling Priscilla coming to a close in her story, Chrysalis moved closer to his sister and put his arm around her shoulders. As she finished speaking, he kissed her on the cheek and thanked her for her gift. The listeners seemed in a trance, almost unable to move for a few moments. The power and mystery of Priscilla's story had them spellbound. Gradually, they pulled themselves back to their normal state, yawning and stretching and looking around. Quietly, they bid each other goodnight and made their way to their respective quarters.

Marguerite looked around at the gathering before her, noticing heavy heads and tired eyes. "And that's what we'll be doing now, dear friends. Make your way to your beds, and I'll see you on the morrow." The tall, gaunt woman rose and moved slowly into the darkness outside the lantern's glow. As the listeners drifted away one by one, a small boy remained behind. When everyone was gone, he sat looking into the flame of the lantern...as if he saw something there, but was not quite sure.

Marguerite watched the boy from the shadows as he stared transfixed into the flame. Slowly, as in a dream, she began to see what he was seeing. Someone in bright, colorful costume was dancing, laughing and leaping about with great abandon. As the vision expanded, there were more dancers, each bringing artistic movement, joy and energetic expression to the scene. She could hear singing midst the laughter, and the sounds lifted her heart and soul. The color, movement and rhythmical pulsing of the vision continued for some time. The old crone and the boy were mesmerized by what they saw.

As the vision faded, the boy yawned, rose and slowly made his way home. Retrieving the lantern, Marguerite turned toward her quarters, with the joyful images of the dancers in her head. She knew that her story was coming to a close, and felt a deep peace at its conclusion.

Chapter Fifteen: Coming Home

The next morning many of the listeners showed up early, as though they sensed a great wonder afoot. Marguerite, herself aglow with the previous night's vision, arrived early as well. She was ready to begin as the crowd settled in. The crone smiled as she looked into the hearts of her listeners, knowing the treasures that lay in store for them for having made this journey. She resumed the telling with a dancing light in her eyes that her audience had not seen before.

♥ The Return of Serai

Serai had been watching all of these events unfold, from her vantage point in the lower realms. With the help of Magus, she had gained powers that allowed her this special vision into the many facets of the story evolving around her.

Long ago, she retreated into the darkness because that was the only way she could be with the blessed beasts and children who were exiled there. Now she was heartened as she watched the courageous companions in Corazon retrieve their lost, frightened and abandoned children from the dungeons and carry them into the light. Others in the castle began to follow suit, as the stories were told and the listeners began to understand the power, healing and joy that could only be acquired by means of the journey to the inner realms.

The day was approaching for Serai's return. She sat quietly now, in her dungeon chambers with her friend Magus.

Since leaving her parents those many years hence, Serai had not aged in body. Her countenance and presence was that of a wise and loving being, and her appearance that of a child.

The wizard spoke.

"Beloved child, you know how you were revered when you once walked the courtyards of Corazon. The people in their confusion failed to see your beautiful essence in all of the precious ones, which is the tragedy that led to the separation and your long exile here below. I am concerned that if you return in your pure and radiant form, others will once again pale in comparison and lose favor in the eyes of those unable to see beyond appearances."

"You are so wise, dear Magus." The sweet melody of Serai's voice went deep into the old wizard's heart, surprising him with a feeling that was unfamiliar of late. "I want the common folk to see the beauty of all of my brothers and sisters, and all of the innocent and powerful beasts. I do not need nor desire adulation, and can easily see the harm it would bring, as you sagely state. What would you suggest? It is clear that my return is imminent."

"You already know that you can appear and speak to the hearts of all, my Serai. Would you be willing to forego your individual existence, and live in and through all those who make an opening for you? Do I ask too much?" The wizard looked slightly worried as he spoke, an unfamiliar expression on his well-lined countenance.

Serai was silent and still. Magus waited. They did not move nor speak for a seemingly interminable period, neither one unfamiliar with stillness and silence.

Stirring finally, Serai looked at Magus and smiled.

"What you speak of is my destiny, and my joy. I prefer living in the way that will allow me to serve the most. I long to look for, find and enter those sacred openings in the hearts, minds and souls of the willing and the true. This is no loss to me, kind Magus. You know the choice I am making, for it is one you have made as well. Like you, I will only rarely reveal my total individual personage, at those times when that is the best way to give my message to those who are ready. My primary existence will be in the quiet inner realms, the soft voices and inclinations that speak to open minds and warm hearts."

Their eyes met, and their steady gaze held. The wizened visage of the old magician softened ever deeper in his love and admiration of the innocent beauty and power of the divine Serai. No more words were needed now. Both knew the path that lay ahead.

♥ Blessing of the Beasts

"We are not alone, you know." Magus lowered his voice slightly with these words, turning ever so slightly toward the shadows outside the ring of light that illumined him and Serai.

"I know." Serai responded.

Then, as if she had made a decision long destined and now come to fruition, she turned directly toward the large shapes looming in the darkness and spoke in a voice that sounded somehow wild and otherworldly.

"Come forth, noble Regalis. Come forth, great Leone. We would have you join us here. It is time that you bring your power from the hidden realms and offer it to those with the breadth of spirit to provide a container for its purposes."

The shadows moved, and a soft rumble subtly shook the rock walls of the ancient chamber. The two great beasts walked slowly toward the child and the wizard. Their massive golden manes were illumined by the candlelight, and momentarily concealed the magnificent form of their muscular bodies.

A ripple of awe ran across the features of the wizard and the child, as the majestic lions were revealed from the shadows in their totality. Their tremendous beauty and power combined with the sweet innocent devotion in their eyes to provide an ecstatic calmness in Magus and Serai.

Serai laughed softly as Regalis gently licked her cheek with his huge, wet tongue. Something between a purr and the rumble of a small earthquake filled the air as she stood and began running her hands through his mane, stroking him behind the ears and along his neck.

Magus, true to form in his playful trickery, had his entire arm around the neck and head of Leone, pulling the great beast into an embrace that would have been a deadly action for another man. Leone rumbled his satisfaction, enjoying the magnificent feeling of close contact with this ancient and powerful wizard.

Turning to Serai, Magus spoke with laughter in his voice as Leone pushed against him like a kitten. "These two are also ready to return, though their full corporeal presence would cause as much alarm and confusion as yours and mine combined. Their fate and mission is like ours, to serve where there is an opening, to enter where invited by a child, woman or man capable of giving expression to their raw, primal energy. They are the reminders of the healthy and necessary animal aspects of our existence, and they challenge us to welcome them without letting them rule."

"And that's where we come in," Serai responded. "They are best in the presence of my love and your wisdom, friend Magus.

"The darkness has been honored, and less fear prevails in the castle Corazon. There are now many there who know these realms well, and have encountered, wrestled and rested with the beasts of their bodies and souls. The doors to the dungeons are open, and the movement between the realms is fluid. Fresh breezes now enter the stagnant regions, releasing energies long stored there. The beasts are no longer dangerous in their isolation, and you and I can watch more closely than ever to insure safety for all. The people are listening to the wisdom of their souls, so that compassion permeates notion and deed."

"Let us be about the business of returning, then," spoke the wizard after a pause. My blessings to you, dear Serai."

"And mine to you, great Magus." Serai blew out the candle and stood.

As the two parted ways, each took a different path into the labyrinth. Regalis walked beside Serai and Leone by Magus.

When the dungeon chamber was empty, a soft glow remained hovering in the air.

Such greatness leaves a footprint, which fades only slowly over time.

♥ Marcelus' Decision

Marcelus woke up early the day following Priscilla's story.

The unfolding events in Corazon were bringing about deep changes in the merchant. He was experiencing unusual emotions that kept him slightly off balance.

The particular feeling opening in his chest on this morning was strong and steady, almost startling in its size and presence. The merchant was relieved to find the sensation slowly morphing into a reassuring confidence regarding what lay before him.

These experiences had become common to Marcelus since he had begun regular sojourns into the lower regions of the castle Corazon. New energy, surges of joy and unexplained feelings of enthusiasm had become more commonplace with each passing week. He was able, over time, to integrate the new emotion into a greater sense of well being.

As was also a frequent occurrence of late, the merchant's thoughts now turned to Samantha. His love and admiration for her had grown consistently over recent months, to the point that it was difficult for him to contain it.

To Marcelus, the statuesque blond woman warrior was more strikingly beautiful every time he saw her. He had actually been somewhat intimidated by her at first, her warrior energy and piercing eyes setting a fear in his heart that stopped any thought of amorous approach.

Lately, however, Samantha had begun to soften. Her power was still there, yet it was somehow deeper and less threatening, as a light and playful spirit emerged in her increasingly radiant countenance.

The two had begun spending more intimate time together in the evenings, taking long walks along the parapet and watching sunsets from the hilltop after an afternoon of horseback riding.

"I've been thinking of asking Samantha to marry me."

Marcelus looked down at his hands as he spoke with Chrysalis over a breakfast of fresh fruit and dry bread in a small café in Aldea.

Without thinking about what he was doing, Chrysalis was suddenly on his feet and striding around the table to embrace his friend. The merchant of light was exuberant to know of the growing love between two of his dearest companions.

"Excellent, my friend! I was wondering when you were going to acknowledge what all about you have seen for some time. Your love for each other is an inspiration and a joy to us all, and I for one will relish the opportunity to celebrate your union with you!"

Marcelus could not suppress the smile that now burst across his face. The quick and spontaneous affirmation from Chrysalis had completely removed the small amount of nervousness he had felt a moment before.

"Thank you, my true and loyal friend. Your support means much to me. Which brings me to another question, albeit somewhat premature. Assuming Samantha will do me the honor of joining me in wedlock, will you honor us by presiding over our ceremony? I can think of no one better suited."

"It will be my privilege, Marcelus. And, in case you haven't noticed, Samantha has been saying 'Yes!' to you with her eyes for months now. All you have to do is ask the question!"

"The master jeweler has crafted us a ring, which was ready last week. I think I am going to ask her tonight," Marcelus responded.

"My blessings to you both, friend. We will talk more of the ceremony as the day of your wedding approaches."

With Chrysalis' words the two friends embraced again, and with hearty pats on the back and big smiles, they parted for the day.

♥ Samantha's Joy

The fluttering in her heart was there again. Samantha worked with the flower in her hair until it opened at just the right angle that its color offset her hair and eyes. "Breathe," she told herself, trying to calm her heart in its unexplained excitement.

For some reason, tonight's dinner with Marcelus felt different, and he did seem a little nervous when he invited her. "I wonder..." she thought, then dismissed the idea.

The knock at her chamber doors reawakened the fluttering, which Samantha worked to control as she opened the door to a Marcelus more handsome than she remembered.

The merchant seemed to stand taller and have a greater sense of stillness in him. When she looked into his eyes, however, they betrayed a tension, a feeling that something important was about to occur.

"It is good to see you, Samantha," Marcelus smiled as he embraced his friend.

"And you, Marcelus!"

As the two left arm in arm, Samantha was surprised to find that they were walking in the wrong direction. All of the dining halls, taverns and eateries were the other way. Now her curiosity was truly peaked.

Opening the door to his own private chambers, Marcelus stood aside and said, "Welcome, my love."

The scene that awaited Samantha stopped her breath, and

touched her heart in such a way that she instantly knew where the fluttering had been coming from.

The lute and violin duo began playing as soon as the door opened, and the breeze from the open door caused the scores of candles surrounding the room to flicker in sequential response. Flowers adorned every archway and opening, the whole scene providing a magnificent heart-shaped frame for the table for two set in its middle.

When she had caught her breath and regained her senses, Samantha turned to express her surprise and appreciation to Marcelus.

He wasn't there!

She looked all around her before hearing his voice from below, "Samantha!"

Looking down, she saw the man she loved down on one knee before her, the beautiful display in the room framing and crowning his countenance.

"Will you honor me by accepting my invitation to marriage?" All of the nervousness was gone from Marcelus now, and his strength filled him as he looked steadily into her eyes.

"Yes!"

The word seemed to leap from her throat as Samantha stepped forward into the rising merchant's arms. The embrace that followed washed both man and woman with a spirit of love so strong that it signaled birth and death, beginning and ending. Much of who they had been was dying in that moment, and new life, new presence was being born. The wedding of two great souls had begun.

As the musicians transitioned into a waltz, the couple's

embrace became a dance, and Marcelus and Samantha swirled around the room in each other's arms, laughing and luxuriating in the greatest joy either had ever known.

At that moment, everyone in the castle felt a growing warmth in their heart. The joy and love of the betrothed couple spread through castle walls, floors and ceilings, enlivening and energizing all those with the opening to receive.

When the delicious dinner of honey-glazed venison and fresh vegetables from the castle garden was consumed and the goblets of fine berry wine drained, Samantha and Marcelus sat across from each other silently, looking deeply into one another's eyes.

Though neither knew it, Serai and Regalis peered from behind Samantha's eyes straight into the gaze of Magus and Leone resting quietly in the back of Marcelus' mind. The great love that was growing between these two created a very large space, into which beauty, grace and magic could easily emerge. The joining of male and female spirit activated a creative force that formed a completion in nature, giving rise to new life in many forms.

All of the children they had once been, the little ones brought up from the darkness below, were now free to be, to become, and to celebrate.

At one moment, the lute player thought he saw children playing and laughing in faint shadows in the corner of the room. When he focused his eyes there, they disappeared. Yet the images of the little ones stayed with him as his fingers played even more lightly across the strings of his instrument, bringing music to the lovers' hearts.

Pausing to drink from her wineskin, Marguerite gave herself a moment to enjoy the sparkling eyes of her listeners, moistened by tears of joy. She noticed that some of the couples were holding hands.

♥ New Life in the Castle Corazon

There was no cause for delay. The festivities began immediately. It was as if everyone in the castle had been waiting for this day, and now they were free to express their joy for Samantha's and Marcelus' union.

Perhaps the most delightful development in the midst of the reverie was the spontaneous eruption of jest and jocularity.

Ever since the children had begun returning from the shadows, light-heartedness and silliness had become more commonplace. Scenes of young ones playing hoops and ball on the lawns outside the castle were common these days. Jesters were showing up in surprising places, just in time to divert disputes that might have otherwise become more serious conflicts.

Laughter could be heard almost everywhere, such that it became as familiar as the sounds of birdsong around the castle towers and surrounding treetops. Smiling faces were so common that a frown was surprising, and a cause for compassionate concern.

"We'll need lots of music, banners, flowers and food!" Chrysalis nearly shouted in his joy to Sebastian and Priscilla. "Will you help me in the preparations?"

"Of course!" The two spoke in enthusiastic unison, then broke into laughter at their spontaneous outburst. "We'll be glad to help!" Sebastian said when he had caught his breath. "You couldn't stop us if you tried!" Priscilla threw in with another laugh.

"And everyone's invited! It is Samantha's and Marcelus' specific request that no one be excluded from the festivities, unless by their own will. We must do all in our power to see that the unwell and infirm have a chance to be there if they're able. It will do them good, and all of us good to see them sharing in our time of joy.

"We will hold the wedding in the castle gardens near the great hall, and the ceremony will be on the steps where all can easily see. This is a grand occasion to celebrate love, marriage and the beauty of lasting friendship!"

As Chrysalis finished speaking, he noticed something new about Priscilla. His sister glanced at Sebastian with an expression he had never seen on her usually serious face. At his last words, "love, marriage and the beauty of lasting friendship," she seemed to blush a little, and glanced at the strong and good Sebastian with a happy and somewhat hopeful look.

As if he knew her feelings without returning her glance, Sebastian smiled as well, pretending to Chrysalis that he was only responding to his words and not to the warmth from Priscilla by his side.

"So! It's settled, then. We'll need to meet regularly as the day approaches, and it's only a fortnight away! I'll see you here again tomorrow, and we'll begin planning in earnest!"

As the two walked away together, their shoulders touching slightly, Chrysalis felt a deep happiness coming from his heart. He realized for the first time that his little sister was now fully a woman, and ready to take a mate. And he could not imagine a better partner for her than his true and steadfast friend Sebastian.

♥ Preparation for The Wedding

It was late in the evening two days before the wedding, and Chrysalis sat with Sebastian over flagons of ale at their favorite tavern. The warrior was surprised by his friend's dark countenance and furrowed brow. He listened quietly as Chrysalis spoke with a slight tremor in his usually calm voice.

"I've never done this before. I have no idea how to proceed.

Marcelus and Samantha have asked me to compose their ceremony, and I agreed before thinking. I know it is part of my privilege as a teacher and spiritual guide in the castle to perform this type of ceremony, but I simply have no experience."

"Will you allow me to speak freely, my friend? I have something to say, and its nature is such that I need your permission before speaking." Sebastian's question surprised Chrysalis, yet he easily consented for his friend to continue.

Feeling the invitation in Sebastian's heart and mind, Magus rose up from within the warrior, so that their thoughts could weave together into one voice.

Chrysalis noticed something like a shimmering wave pass across Sebastian's face. He barely had time to wonder at the change when his friend began to speak in a voice slightly deeper and more resonant than before.

"You were born for this, my friend. You are meant to guide spiritual processes and convene sacred gatherings. It is in your destiny, and you have known it since you were a child. Yes, you went astray, and who among us does not? That is part of life's journey. We receive our blessing, experience our inspiration, and in our youthful exuberance we fly off in one direction or another. Then life's wisdom redirects us to a deeper understanding of that original purpose, a deeper knowing of our true mission. The misguided folly of youth doesn't mean your first inspiration was wrong, it simply means you need the wisdom of life experience before you can give full fruition to your vision. You have a sobriety now that was missing before. That sobriety will keep you and others safe and grounded as you move closer to the light in your spiritual mission of teaching and leading."

A silence followed Sebastian's words, long enough that he wondered if he had offended Chrysalis.

At last, Chrysalis spoke. "You honor me with your wisdom and your candor, Sebastian, and I thank you. I feel in my heart that you are right in what you say. My deepest wish is to help without doing harm. I know that I have gifts, and with the help of solid, grounded friends like you, I feel I can use them wisely."

Feeling thus settled in his role, Chrysalis began designing the ceremony in earnest, in consultation with Samantha and Marcelus.

The day before the ceremony, dark clouds filled the skies over Corazon and the roll of distant thunder brought the prospect of rain. Although it had been hot and still for several days, that was preferable to a downpour on the outdoor wedding about to take place.

In the middle of the afternoon, more thunder and a little lightning was followed by a steady, soaking rain. It lasted for about an hour, and subsided.

What followed was a blessing no less than the smiles of friends, the beautiful music and the radiant flowers. After the storm, the air was cool and crisp, and the next morning dawned with sharp colors and brilliant light. The storm had washed away the dust of the previous day's dry heat and energized the atmosphere in a way only a good storm can. They could not have asked for better weather for the ceremony.

Though they truly had little time to prepare, all were ready. Chrysalis wrote the ceremony, Marcelus had the ring made, and all of the maids and groomsmen were dressed appropriately and knew their roles. The parents and families of the bride and groom were gathered, and pleased with the arrangements.

The bride and groom were attired in their finest. Marcelus was striking in his elegant gold embroidered purple tunic with billowy sleeves, navy tights, sky blue scarf and black velvet hat with violet feathers.

Yet it was Samantha's bridal gown that stole the show, as well it should.

A train extending five cubits at her back offset the delicate lines formed by exquisitely crafted lace patterning a mosaic of magnificent intricacy from her veil to the hem of her garment. Strands of gold and silver had been carefully woven into the lace designs subtly depicting swans in flight, such that her garment sparkled and shone with the slightest of movements. Her long wavy hair was down and full, framing her face with elegant curls and swirls.

Beyond the dress, however, it was Samantha's radiant joy that most enhanced her beauty. Both bride and groom were smiling broadly, as if on the verge of bursting into laughter. Yet the seemingly boundless joy was held ever so gracefully in the quiet poise of these two exceptional human beings.

A hush fell over the crowd as Marcelus and Samantha walked slowly together toward Chrysalis on the top step in front of the great hall. Enchanting music wafted down from an ensemble on the great hall balcony overlooking the castle gardens and the seated guests. The four-member troupe played psaltery, rebec, lute and crumhorn, combining to create an effect perfectly suited to the occasion. A slight breeze moved Samantha's hair about her face, and gently ruffled the feather on Marcelus' hat as they arrived and stood on a step below Chrysalis.

♥The Ceremony

Basking in the radiance of the beautiful couple before him, Chrysalis addressed his audience, saying,

"We gather today in great joy, to celebrate the love of this fine man and this fine woman. We honor their union, and their decision to publicly profess their undying love in the presence of all who know them. This is a marriage of great souls, and a marriage of many dimensions. In the union of masculine and feminine, we find the joining of sacred darkness with light, change with constancy. We now bring together Marcelus and Samantha, night and day, summer and winter, spring and fall. We honor the hallowed union of earth and sky, fire and water, man and woman.

"This ceremony is beyond us, and it emerges from us. Each one gathered here offers an element invaluable to this noble gentleman and elegant lady as they embark on their blessed journey of matrimony. Together we acknowledge and invite the great mystery of Life, the presence of the very Creator, to join us in this moment."

Chrysalis allowed a silence to fill the space following his words. All present sensed a heightening; a slight uplifting of spirit, as if indeed something unseen yet powerfully felt had entered.

"We know that it is through grace that love is honored and cherished beyond judgment and reaction. Together today we envision such grace in this marriage of Marcelus and Samantha, so that they may know they are never alone, and that their love does not solely depend on them. The love of true lasting commitment is greater than what we can create; yet it is our willingness and loyal devotion that invites and maintains it over time.

"May you, Marcelus, and you, Samantha, welcome this divine grace as your third partner in marriage. May you come to know, honor and cultivate this celestial presence that is born within and sustains the love you have for each other. May this sacred guest be your constant spiritual focus, that you do not ask godliness of each other. Allow, enjoy and celebrate the humanity of your partner, and ask no more of him, of her...than to be who he...who she...was born to be.

"What say you to each other on this occasion?" Chrysalis waited for the couple to recite their vows, which they had composed together.

As he saw their eyes meet, Chrysalis felt a jolt of energy surge through his chest. Samantha and Marcelus' love for each other was so great that it seemed to emanate outward, touching all present and extending beyond even to those out of sight and earshot.

Marcelus spoke first. His voice was strong and clear, with a steadiness underlying his words that gave no doubt regarding his commitment to their meaning.

> "I commit to preserve the integrity of your spirit
> I honor the person that you are
> I choose you, as you are
> I love you, as you are.
>
> Our love, our relationship has been blessed and sanctified.
> God has entered here, in this space between us
> In this vast, mysterious, beautiful realm
> Invisible to the eye
> Yet palpable to the body, heart, mind and soul.
>
> It is in this holy place that I wed you
> This place not of your making
> Nor of mine
> This place that was created
> Through the silent merging of our souls,
>
> Together now, at long last.
> I love you, and would not control you
> I long for you, and will not cling to you
> I hunger for the sweet essence of your touch
> And I will not take from you.
>
> My commitment is to the enhancement
> Of your life on this Earth.
> My commitment is to be devoted, loyal steward
> Of this sacred, beautiful essence of divine love
> That moves silently, powerfully
> Between the shores of our souls.

> I choose you, as my wife
> I choose to be your husband
>
> I commit to being a healthy, happy man
> Body, heart mind and soul
> In my role as your husband
>
> I choose to marry you."

Then, as if the words had never before been spoken, Samantha spoke the same vows to Marcelus in a voice equally focused, clear and resonant. No one present could doubt the strength of their commitment and love for each other.

With tears in his eyes and a slight catch in his throat, Chrysalis said, "And with these inspired and well spoken words, I now declare you to be husband and wife."

In a movement slow in its elegance and care, Marcelus reached up and lightly held Samantha's cheeks in both his hands. As he leaned to kiss her, she rose to meet him. As their lips met in ecstatic union, those gathered and watching knew they had the rare privilege of observing great love in its most intimate expression.

As the moment passed and the couple turned toward the crowd, with a spontaneous gesture of joy and exhilaration they threw up their arms and shouted together, "Let the festivities begin!"

♥ Celebration and Ongoing Joy

The audience burst into applause, the musicians started playing a lively tune, and dancers leapt spontaneously into exuberant movement.

The celebration that followed went on for three days. The revelers were so caught up in the laughter, good food, drink, dance and song that they hardly noticed Marcelus and

Samantha's departure. The couple quietly made their way to a waiting carriage on the evening of the second day, which spirited them away to a mountain lodge perfectly suited for their nuptial rites over the ensuing hours and days.

Ensconced in the comfort of their private haven, Marcelus and Samantha made love with every fabric of their being. Their ecstatic pleasure and euphoria permeated body and soul, emanating from man and woman to merge and fill every space within and far beyond their physical presence. Whether joined in sexual embrace, holding hands as they walked on the mountaintop, or merely looking into each other's eyes across a sumptuous meal, their lovemaking was without pause.

Back at the castle, the celebration continued for days. In a realm only Magus and Serai could observe, the emanating waves of passion from the couple's conjugal culminations extended into the hearts and loins of the revelers, sparking new romance and fueling the festivities beyond what Corazon had ever known. Perhaps central among these were Priscilla and Sebastian, now an inseparable pair whose love was evident to all.

Samantha and Marcelus' demonstration of integrity, individuality and commitment in marriage served as a powerful example for all who knew them. Both were distinct autonomous beings, complete and whole in many ways. They chose to marry out of love and desire, not from need or insufficiency. This bonding of such powerful individuals set a tone for relationship that became a model to which many would aspire.

Marguerite paused, and asked for the wineskin. After stretching and shifting around for comfort, she and her listeners were ready to resume. The joy and love of this segment of the story had energized the gathering to a heightened level of awareness, and they felt as if they could move into the crone's tale and live there always.

♥ A New Presence

As these wondrous events transpired, changes occurred at many levels in Corazon. When conflict arose, for example, a new element was present that had not been there before.

Disputes in the marketplace or in the marriage bed, at games or in serious competition invited a fresh potency so electric and real that many were motivated toward resolution who would formerly have fought to a bitter end.

"It is Regalis and Leone at their best," Magus remarked to Serai. "The robust atmosphere in the castle these days has invited your love and my wisdom where before only the hostility of the solitary beast would reside. The great lions do not seem to want to work separately from us, no more than we do from them. They give us the ground and passion to complement our more ethereal offerings of love and wizardry. Look now, those lads playing fox and geese are showing what I speak of."

"You cheated! I saw you take one of my geese when you thought I wasn't looking! Put it back, or I'll..." The first boy tensed his upper body and clinched his fists.

"You'll what?" The other boy challenged.

The two were rearing up, ready to start swinging, when something stopped them. Simultaneously, both caught a flicker of something in the eye of the other that brought them up short.

As if in a waking dream, the two lads saw an image that would stay with them for the rest of their lives.

A magnificent lion stood calmly between an old wizard and a little girl. The contrast of wisdom in the man, innocence in the child and fierceness in the lion brought a blend of power and compassion to the minds and hearts of the boys. They felt a sobriety now, that totally calmed their ire.

Both were in a mild state of shock over what they had seen, but had no words for talking about it.

"Okay, you're right," said the first boy when he had regained some sense of composure. "I thought I could get away with it, but you caught me. I'll sacrifice a turn as a penalty, if that appeases you." He spoke with a slight smile on his face, further easing the tension with his opponent and friend.

After a moment and a deep breath, the other boy responded. "That's fair. But don't do it again, or we're done here!" He too could not keep from smiling. One of the things he liked about his friend was that he liked to push the edges and keep things stirred up. They had had their share of scuffles in the past but remained close regardless. Both were committed to preserving their friendship.

"Yes, I see," Serai remarked. "Their glimpse of the other's power and grace interrupted the cycle to violence.

"My hope and prayer, good Magus, is that such a spirit will grow and spread throughout the castle and ultimately throughout the land. It is time for all to awaken to the magnificence, beauty and power that each possesses."

"I agree, dear Serai. I agree."

Marguerite's smile seemed to rise up from her heart with a will of its own. The joy she felt at the culmination of the story, and the knowledge of what was to come filled her with a sense of ecstatic expectation. Showing her emotion only in her eyes, she bid her audience good day. "Join me here again tomorrow night when you have had your evening repast. A special surprise awaits you for the conclusion of our story."

Chapter Sixteen: Reunion

The crone arrived early, and built a large fire to ward off the chill of night. She stood still and silent in the flicker of firelight as her listeners approached and found their places. When all were settled, she spoke. "And now, dear hearts, I want to introduce you to those very ones you have come to know and love over the past months of our gatherings." A ripple of shock and disbelief passed across the faces of her listeners.

As Marguerite finished speaking, a tall striking form emerged from the shadows beyond reach of fire glow.

"I give you…Magus!"

♥ Magus Speaks

A collective breath was taken in by the crowd as the Magus of their minds, the image from the story in their heads materialized before their very eyes. The statuesque, wizened magician was clad in a dark gray hooded robe, held together in front with a carved wooden clasp displaying the image of a majestic oak. His steady eyes seemed to look at all of those gathered at the same time. Each of the listeners felt as if he were addressing them personally when he spoke.

The wizard smiled ever so slightly and raised his hand, to put his stunned observers at ease.

"What you are about to experience is something you have been prepared for. Some of you may already have realized that the great lady Marguerite is a woman of significant power and ability. Her powers are similar to mine. She has brought you to this point, and together we will take you the rest of the way. If you were not ready for the journey, you would not be here.

"The wizard you see before you is the wizard of your mind. I am your creation, yet I am your guide to realms beyond your wildest imaginings. I grew within you as the story progressed, yet I existed before you knew me. And now we are ready to journey together. I am a doorway to the deeper realms of yourself and beyond. I offer you the keys to your own power and wisdom, and to the power and wisdom of the Great One who is the Creator of us all.

"Consult me. Let me help you. I am always here, waiting to assist you in your life journey. I am your brilliance, your magic, the wizardry of your mind. And I can bring you help from beyond, when the time is right. Trust me, trust yourself, trust your Creator to guide you to the fulfillment of your mission and purpose."

As he finished speaking, Magus dropped his head ever so slightly as a gesture of respect, and stepped back a little way into the shadows.

Marguerite spoke.

"Now prepare yourselves, dear ones."

With no further words, Marguerite turned toward the shadows and slowly waved her long arm into the darkness as if she was opening a curtain to reveal a grand and majestic treasure.

Gradually, the images of five beings began to form before the astonished eyes of the listeners. There before them, at the edge of the shadows, facing the light, were Samantha, Marcelus, Sebastian, Priscilla and Chrysalis. Each appeared exactly as the listeners had pictured them in their minds during the story, making it seem as if they knew them personally and well.

Then both Marguerite and Magus turned together toward another direction. Everyone watched and waited. Slowly, the image of two lions and a small girl-child appeared, as they walked ceremoniously into the circle of light. The child had one of her hands buried deeply in the fur of the lion nearest her. The smile on Serai's face brought a profound sense of peace and joy to the hearts and minds of all those privileged to see her.

Marguerite now appeared more radiant and beautiful than her listeners had ever seen her. Her skin was translucent, permeated with light that rippled as she moved and spoke.

"These are the aspects of your soul, beloved ones. They represent the many and varied components of your being. Hear them now, as they tell you who they are to you, and how they can help you become who you were born to be."

♥ Marcelus Speaks

As if punctuating her sentence with his footstep, Marcelus stepped forward on Marguerite's last word. Smiling slightly, the handsome, dark-haired merchant addressed his audience.

"Life is a transaction. In every action and interaction, something is given and something is returned. While some temporarily gain more than they give or give more than they receive, the laws of nature will have their way and balance will be restored. Seek balance in all of your transactions. Look for fair deals, in which the gain is mutual. When you act in accordance with the law of balance, it will work for you. When you act against it, it may seem at times to be your adversary.

"Be a good negotiator. Hold true to your values, and offer only your best. Expect and hold out for an adequate return on your investment. Be strong in this, and do not mistake your own loss for kindness or generosity. When you are truly generous, your gain is far greater than what you give. Take excellent care of yourself in all regards, and from the abundant harvest of your investments you will have much to share with your loved ones and with the world at large.

"Be neither greedy nor self-depreciating. When you seek to achieve a balanced exchange in all that you do, your gains will be consistent and abundant beyond your dreams. This world is generous with the wise and fair, and harsh with the ignorant and greedy, however temporary illusions may indicate otherwise.

"Be wise in your giving. Doing for those who can do for themselves is neither love nor generosity. Giving from your harvest to those who can grow their own will cripple them, and they will turn against you in bitterness. Make your investments where they will do the most good, for you, the recipients and the larger systems around you.

"This world has abundant resources for all. Yet it is a powerful teacher, and it teaches us that we must be astute, circumspect, open, flexible and steadfast in our strategies, skills and values.

"Know that what you need is already provided, and do the work to open the door to your receiving. This is indeed an abundant Universe. When you work according to the laws of nature, seeking balance and positive outcomes for all, you work in partnership with the Great One and the Creator of all things. In this way, all of your dreams will be realized."

♥ Sebastian Speaks

As Marcelus spoke his last words, Sebastian approached to stand by his side. Marcelus turned to meet the eyes of his warrior friend, the two nodded slightly to each other, and Marcelus stepped back.

Sebastian's formidable size and massive build created a subtle ripple of awe among the listeners. Yet when his voice reached their ears, its tone soothed any trepidation they may have felt.

"Protect yourselves, and do not become prisoners to your own self-made walls. Guard the sacred space of your being, your home and your loved ones, and know that true protection can only emanate from the knowledge of your own divine nature.

"Know your guards well, so they do not become hyper-vigilant and obsessed in the performance of their duties. Your guards and protectors will do their job, with or without your awareness. Left to their own devices, however, they can become destructive. Using whatever means they have at their disposal, your protectors may shield you with substances, and you will become a slave to the substance. Without your wisdom, the interior guards of your body and mind will use your emotions, your impulses and destructive behaviors to separate you from the forces that seem to threaten you. If you let them, these blind protectors will separate you from your loved ones, from your health, and even from life itself.

"Your guards and protectors need your help in order to protect you well and without doing harm. Spend the time to learn all the ways in which you defend yourself, and bring your wisdom and good heart to these places. Working in conjunction with the many aspects of your radiant self, your protectors' power is absolute.

"Develop your mind and body to be strong and flexible. Create fluid movement throughout your being, so that in one moment you can be unyielding as a fortress, and in the next as open and responsive as a mountain stream.

"There is great wisdom in your body. It will awaken and emerge as you care for, develop and trust it. Your body, mind and soul are one.

"All of the protection you need is with you in each moment. You have but to develop the skill to activate and step aside. Stand firm and relax. Be an oak, then a sapling. Your strength is neither in your yielding nor your unyielding. It is in your fluid movement within and among your various capacities.

"The source of your protection ultimately comes neither from your strength nor your skill. These are essential to your functioning; yet they are not the origin of the power that guards you. Your ultimate safety is a force field that emanates from the core of your being. Its strength depends on your love and devotion to yourself, and to the source of your being. Recognize your own wounds, innocence, vulnerability and beauty, and devote yourself to the care of your soul.

"Your self-care enables the greatest power of all—the power of love. From this core, this essential nature, the presence of the Creator is evoked on your behalf.

"Remember, you are so much more than you know."

♥ Samantha Speaks

As if to illustrate the truth of Sebastian's last words, Samantha stepped forward before he had finished speaking. Bowing slightly to his audience, Sebastian backed away to the edge of the shadows with his friends.

Firelight danced in the radiant waves of Samantha's golden hair. Her piercing gaze held the attention of the listeners. She paused a moment to smile at each of those present.

"You know my journey, and my struggles. You know of my sword, my fury and my fear. I come now to speak to you of your journey, in hopes that my story will help you along your way.

"Here is what I have learned.

"There is a force inside you whose purpose is to protect you from actual or would-be offenders. Unlike those forces of which Sebastian spoke, however, this one is sharp, piercing, penetrating and aggressive by nature. Like the sword, its job is to make a point, to cut through barriers, and to ward off foes and violators.

"To accomplish its purpose, this protector is willing to do harm, and even to take life. That is why you must befriend it, so that it is in service to your highest good. Without your conscious attention, this protector can easily become blind and destructive in its efforts to protect you from pain. It is not evil, though it can seem so if neglected, undeveloped, or cultivated for destructive ends.

"Become knowledgeable and skilled in the use of your anger. Anger is the fuel, the emotional energy empowering the sword to do its work. Use your anger and your sword in conjunction with your good heart and wisdom and you will have a powerful ally and a loyal warrior-servant always by your side.

"To accomplish this, you must know the depth and breadth of your entire being. You must know your animal nature and your capacity for wildness and abandon. If you do not traverse and become familiar with these realms of your inner domain, they can be inhabited by dangerous and caustic elements that would as soon harm you as others."

A low growl accompanied the approach of Leone and Regalis from the shadows. Each took his place by Samantha's side, standing at ready with that uniquely feline expression that danced between playful and fierce. Without looking down, the warrior slowly moved her hands into the thick fur of the lions' massive manes.

"These two glorious beasts represent the power each of you possesses in your animal nature. Ignore them, fight with them, attempt to control them or turn them to stone and they will be left to their own devices. With no ill intent, they will forget their original purpose of protection, and move almost exclusively into destructive patterns.

"They will show up in your blind rages and attack your loved ones, leaving you to pick up the pieces afterward. If they cannot find release in that way, they may pierce your organs with their teeth and claws, transforming themselves into toxicity and disease. Their original purpose is to protect, yet without your conscious awareness and regulation they can all too easily become purely destructive.

"They are much like your children. They need your attention and your guidance in order to develop well and become the best they can be.

"And they are your guides. All of the animals are mirrors, reflecting your own diverse and beautiful nature. Let their innocent, fierce vulnerability reveal the unclaimed gold in your shadow realms.

"And care well for the temple of your body and mind. The more clear, open, serene and loving the inner sanctum of your soul, the more potent, fierce and efficient will be the lions at your gates.

"When you learn to love your primal nature and develop these forces for the common good, you will become magnificent. Discover the beauty of the beasts in your soul and recognize that their power is your own. When you learn to listen to them, to walk, stand and play with them, their superb essence will permeate your entire being, giving you life and energy you never dreamed possible."

At this point, Samantha kneeled between Leone and Regalis, so that her golden mane was framed by theirs. The listeners were struck by what they saw. For a brief moment, the eyes of the three were the same. They saw the intelligence and deep wisdom of the woman in the eyes of the lions, and the wild beauty of the lions in the eyes of the woman.

"You could not see this if it were not in you," Samantha spoke quietly as she rose to a standing position once again.

"Stand up for yourself. Speak out against what you perceive as wrong, and act forcefully in what you perceive as just and good. Honor yourself, your warrior spirit and the wild beauty of your soul. You will learn by your choices, and over time your actions will become ever more true.

"Search deep in your heart and soul and find the truth that only you can express, and do not let anything stop you from speaking it. Discover the gift that is yours to give and devote the fierce and indomitable spirit of your heart and loins to its offering. Uncover the purpose that is your very reason for being, and devote your warrior spirit to its fulfillment. Use your sword to penetrate the clouds of confusion, self-doubt and fear and move steadily into the vision revealed to you as your personal and individual mission in life."

A ripple of laughter moved through the crowd as Regalis leaned his head into Samantha's leg, almost knocking her off balance. Laughing with them, Samantha turned with her furry friends and the three resumed their places on the edge of darkness, facing the light.

♥ **Chrysalis Speaks**

After only a brief pause, Chrysalis stepped slowly forward and took his place before the audience of listeners. Feeling great joy at being part of such an event, he spoke with energy and enthusiasm.

"Claim your light. Recognize your greatness, your wisdom, your ability to teach and lead. Know that each of you is unique and special in your own way. Hold your head high and rise into the best and most noble aspects of your being. Identify all those you have admired and held above yourself and recognize that their qualities reside in you; else you would not be able to perceive them. Invite each and every great one you have known to live and express symbolically through you, adding their essence to the offering only you can bring.

"And guard against the intoxication of too much light. The lure of the light is great, and it can pull you away from the deep, dark and rich colors of your soul. Cultivate the inner light of your true nature so that it may illumine the dark and uncharted realms of your body, mind and heart. This will ground you to your true nature and to the Earth, restoring your sacred sobriety and the balance that can be threatened with excessive light.

"Be wary of those who may project their light onto you. However good their intentions, they are giving you something that belongs to them, and they will resent you for having it. When you allow others to hold you above, the laws of nature will require that they take you down. When you are firmly planted in the ground of your being and your spirit is focused on the light of your essence, no one can lift you up or take you down.

"Guard against the inflated sense of self-importance and feelings of entitlement that go with success, beauty, accomplishment and talent. These are toxic states of being that will pollute your awareness and blind you to essential realities in your life and relationships.

"Know that there is a child within you who longs to be acknowledged, adored and cherished. Acknowledge, adore and cherish this child within you, and do not become that child asking these things of the world around you.

"Recognize your strengths and weaknesses. Do not shy away from facing your greatness or your failings. Look deep into your inner being, and you will find there the beauty and the beast of your soul. Embrace all that you find, and these energies will be integrated into a whole that allows you to express from your natural wisdom and grace.

"You are as good as the best, and no better than the worst. You are magnificent and insignificant. Hovering among these paradoxical truths you will find freedom. And in this freedom you will find the unfolding mystery of who you are and who you are becoming."

♥ Priscilla Speaks

Chrysalis continued with, "I have spoken to you of the shadow within the light, and now you are to learn of the light within the shadow. I present to you...Priscilla."

Chrysalis stepped outside the ring of firelight, and the listeners noticed for the first time that all of the members of the group before them had disappeared. Only Marguerite remained, who explained calmly, "They are still here. They have retreated further into the darkness out of respect to your next speaker. Wait quietly, dear ones. The shadows must be honored before they will offer their gifts."

A strong silence pervaded the crone and the circle of listeners. Even the fire became quiet, as the flame retreated slightly from a growing presence in the shadows.

As if she had been standing there all along, the image of Priscilla was suddenly before them. Dressed in her customary dark hooded cloak, the steady young woman peered at her audience from behind mysterious and intense eyes. Her slight build was offset by a formidable presence that seemed to speak of a power beyond her physical stature.

When she spoke, her voice brought a strange combination of comfort and foreboding. All of the listeners felt as if they had heard her speaking many times before.

"I will speak to you of the outcast, the overlooked and neglected within you and among you. I guide you to the gold in your shadow, the light in the depths of the darkness, the value in the hidden places of your soul.

"I invite you to look on the other side of appearances to find the beauty extending beyond what can be measured with the eyes. I invite you to see with the vision of your soul, with which you can view the art of the simple and the mundane.

"My domain is that of the wounded and frightened children, the unsightly and disfigured, the odd and the different, the rejected and excluded. I embrace the shadow realms, into which many precious beasts and children retreat to hide from judgment, disdain and fear. Many of them become wild and dangerous there, out of despair and the need for protection. Yet the tenderness is always present, within the shadows.

"This is a creative realm, where a spark is ignited that has nothing to do with approval, recognition or measuring up. This a realm of death and rebirth, retreat and return, immersion and emergence."

Slowly, each of the listeners became aware of movement around Priscilla's skirts. Small shadowy beings gathered within and around the hems of the young woman's robe. One by one, as they settled into their places, the children peeked out from behind Priscilla's skirts to peer at the audience.

"These are the shadow children. They are the hurt and frightened ones, the misfits and the outcasts. Each has value and beauty, and it is only your steady attendance and love that will invite their story and their essence into your life. These children live inside each of us. They represent aspects of our precious and vulnerable inner nature, and they must be honored, heard, nurtured and cared for.

"When you have the courage and the vision to go into the deeper and darker aspects of your inner realms, you will derive the value that these wounded ones bring. The stories they have to tell you are your own stories. They will speak to you of your loneliness, your sorrow and your shame. They will tell you of the times when you were not seen, honored and acknowledged for the beautiful being that you are. They will show you the images of your despair and suffering, as you gain the strength of spirit to face them.

"They carry the wounds of violation. They represent memories of the times when you were a victim of people and circumstances beyond your control. They need you to come and find them and tell their stories. They need you to be strong and protect them from further violation. They are the reason for the protectors. Their wounds and fear are the fuel for your anger.

"These dark realms are magnetic and seductive. Do not allow yourself to be pulled into the perceived power of vengeance for the wrongs done to these precious ones. Become the avenger and you will only create more victims. Justice is done when you enter the essence of your own unbound joy, and this will only happen when you have become still enough to listen to the stories of the children.

"They will be heard, whether you choose to listen or not. It is better for you and for them if you make the choice to hear them of your own accord and will.

"Each of these children will give you a gift of energy and joy when you embrace them and offer your love and protection. All that is asked of you is your unwavering presence in the face of their pain, despair, sorrow and fear. The power of your unconditional love is all that is needed to heal these wounds. To feel this love deeply you must understand what happened, who was responsible, and who was not responsible. The wounds of childhood are never the fault of the children, yet many of these precious ones carry shame for what has happened. It is up to you to set these accounts straight.

"They need you and you need them. You have the strength, understanding, knowledge and life experience that will provide them with the security of a new life outside the dungeons of their memories. They have the childlike innocence, purity of intention, vulnerability and tenderness that will warm your heart and free your soul from captivity."

With a slight smile, Priscilla looked down. She opened her cloak to encompass all of the little ones present, and each tiny form disappeared into the darkness of its folds. And then Priscilla was gone.

♥ Serai Speaks

The silent stillness that followed Priscilla was strong. As the listeners waited, they noticed the flame of the fire growing brighter again, as Marguerite raised her head to address them.

"And now for the ending of your inner journey, and the beginning of your true awakening.

"Serai."

A hush fell over the small gathering. This time even Marguerite disappeared into the shadows. Minutes passed, as a silence grew slowly within the heart of each listener. Every man, woman and child present began to experience a peace beyond what they had ever known. And in the deep inner essence of that peace, a voice spoke:

"I speak to you from within your heart, because that is my true home. As I tell you of myself, I am speaking of who you are.

"I am joy. I am love. I am a doorway to the divine origins of your soul. I am your spiritual essence. I am creativity. I am radiant light. I am the memory of your connection with your true spiritual home. I am the memory of your connection with your Creator."

Upon hearing the voice of Serai from within, the listeners had spontaneously closed their eyes.

As they opened them again, one by one, each beheld a vision that would remain with them always.

The beautiful Serai of their imaginary world slowly materialized before them. A soft, radiant, golden light emanated from her shimmering presence.

From time to time as they watched the glowing child standing serenely before them, the vague outline of Magus seemed to appear around her, as if Serai were somehow a part of the wizard. Then a moment later it would be the subtle image of Marguerite that framed the radiant child. And then one by one, the silhouette of each of the companions, Marcelus, Samantha, Sebastian, Chrysalis and Priscilla appeared to surround the bright image of Serai.

She continued to speak in the hearts and minds of the listeners, in tones that permeated and soothed every fabric of their being.

"I am both innocent and wise. I am new born, and I am the oldest part of you. I am vulnerable, fragile and powerful beyond the reach of your knowing.

"Imagine me as a doorway to worlds beyond your life experience yet relevant to all that you are.

"I represent your beginning as a child in this world. And when you return to me as an adult on your inner journey, I represent the beginning of the final phase of your life. From this moment forward, you will steadily realize your beauty and greatness, and you will grow into more humility than you have known or experienced.

"I am the key that opens the doorway to your divinely inspired purpose in life. I hold the memory of who you really are and who you were born to be.

"Although you can hear and see me now, I will not always be so readily within your reach. You are still susceptible to the clouds of fear, pain and anger. Your vision and inner knowing can still be impaired by the shadows of confusion, self-doubt and distraction. The journey you have made to this point will be made again and again, until it is a well-worn path in your inner realms.

"Each day brings a new opportunity to connect with me, within yourself and in the hearts and minds of all those you meet. And you will meet many merchants, wizards, warriors and artists on your way. You will encounter the beasts and children in their many forms, and some will be easier to love than others.

"The journey will continue. All I ask is that you do not forget me, or how you came to this place. Remember that I am here, and that I represent your essence, your true nature.

"And remember all those you met on your way to this place in your story. Each one has a great gift to offer you. Their gifts are so important, that your progress on your journey will be interrupted until you receive them. Do not despair, however lost you may feel at times. Remember the light in the depths of your being. It is always there. I am always here.

"And remember that you found me on your sojourn through the darkness. Honor the sacred shadow realms, so that you can know the pure radiance of the light.

"I have no favorites, yet I am most drawn to those who quietly create an opening for me.

"Recognize that illusions of beauty and power may hide the greatest wounds of all. At times the strongest need is in the hearts of those who seem to have no needs. Develop your inner vision until you can see beyond the veils and illusions that would hide the truth from your eyes.

"Be wise, and become all that you were meant to be. The gifts you have been given are beyond the measure of your mind. Your greatest challenge in life is to identify, develop and utilize those gifts to their fullest capacity. In this way you will find the peace, the joy and the deep satisfaction your heart so desires.

"And finally, remember the mystery. Be comfortable with your questions, for they are your guides to the ever-opening magnificence of the Universe."

♥ Marguerite, Raconteur Extraordinaire

Marguerite began to materialize where Serai had been standing, and slowly the image of the radiant child faded into the heart of the beloved crone. The storyteller's words seemed to come from all around the listeners, as she began to speak once again.

"Loyal listeners, I thank you for your gracious reception of my story. It is your story, our story, the same story and completely different for each one of us. Find your story, the one only you can tell for only you have lived it. We all need to hear your story. It contains your heart, your soul, the divine spark that we can only witness through you.

"Your inner cast of characters awaits you. These excellent essences of you can only be given full expression as you explore the singular ways in which they manifest through your magnificence. You are individual, and you are many. At the ultimate reaches of your inner universe you access the collective being of which we are all a part.

"The greatest risk in your life is thinking yourself small and limited. Everyone you have ever admired or respected is but a reflection of who you can become. Were it otherwise, you would not have felt admiration for their greatness. Your emotions are your guide to your inner light, the creative source of all you have ever dreamed of. Use your imagination as the eyes and ears of your inner Magus, and find your way through the mystery and to the majesty of you.

"And on your way, you will meet the monsters who have terrified you in the inner and outer worlds. Do not be fooled by their disguises. They are but misguided protectors, warriors and beasts gone astray, and they are in need of your understanding and your loving embrace. They have tremendous energy to offer you. Every perceived weakness, failing or shame is but a treasure waiting to be discovered. You will find your greatest value in the meeting place between your joy and sorrow, in the dynamic explosion of the peace that is your true home.

"Your story, your life experience, is your roadmap to all you have ever wanted to become. It is with you all of the time, as the foundation of your character. Ignore your story and you may find yourself lost in its labyrinth of images and emotions, caught in its projections on the world around you. Work with your story and it will give you the keys to the treasure houses of your inner and outer worlds.

"And in conclusion, dear ones, I say to you that you are author of your story from this point forward. You need not review every detail of your past. Only mine the gold from your storehouse of life experience, that you may use its brilliance in creating your future. Your attention is your mechanism of power and creativity. What you give your attention to grows and becomes a part of your story. There is much to choose from as you search in your mind moment-by-moment, day-by-day. So choose wisely.

"It is my hope for you that your choices will allow the beauty of your essence to come forth in its full glory. This essence remains virtually untouched by your story, and provides a glimpse of the divine spark that originates all life.

"Focus on the exquisite order and artistry of your inner and outer worlds, and you will be one of the great artists of all time.

Your medium of expression is your very life itself, and there is a longing in each of us to see the radiant soul that is you."

The stately and dignified Marguerite paused, and bowed her head slightly. Turning to her side she gestured with extended arm and open hand to all of her companions, visible now in the light of inner and outer fires.

♥ Divine Relationship

"It is not through any one of us that you will find your way home to fulfillment. We are all in relationship, with each other and with you. It is through relationship that you will fully come to this life. It is not our separate existence that brings us into complete expression. It is in and through our connection that we find our true voice."

As the raconteur uttered these mysterious and powerful words, the image of Serai appeared once again in her heart region. Samantha became visible on her right, and Sebastian on her left. Marcelus peered at the listeners over her right shoulder, and Priscilla over her left. A glow of light surrounded Marguerite's head, and the face of Chrysalis appeared just above her. At moments, the visage of Magus seemed to peer through Marguerite's countenance. The listeners were beginning to see that all of these characters could be part of one whole, complete person.

A feeling of silent awe and deep appreciation grew within the gathering, as each listener experienced the combined presence of these great souls.

"We give you but a reflection of your own diversity, your own richness and beauty. Let this vision show you who you are, and who you can be."

The voice that spoke through Marguerite was different somehow, as if it contained the essence of all of the voices of the divine messengers.

In conversations that followed this event, the listeners discovered that they did not all remember the same images or sequence of appearances. Some reported that they had seen Marcelus and Samantha step forward, appearing side by side in the garb of a king and queen. One of these was Aurelius, who stated emphatically, "The merchant Marcelus and the warrior Samantha stood side by side as they had at the marriage altar. Yet now they were adorned in the raiment of royalty. Both wore majestic crowns of gold, befitted with dazzling jewels. Their robes flowed elegantly about their forms, which combined with their regal posture and expression to give no doubt as to their sovereignty."

The boy child Marguerite once held in her arms during the storytelling spoke next. "I saw the wizard Magus and Marguerite standing side by side as king and queen, yet in my eye they were radiant in only their normal garb."

His mother laughed and added, "And I saw Chrysalis and his sister Priscilla side by side, showing divine and regal partnership as brother and sister. I think that each of us saw what best befits our journey and our readiness for learning. Perhaps that is what the wise Marguerite would say if she were here."

Her son smiled and looked up at his mother, saying, "She is here, mother. I just heard her speaking."

BIBLIOGRAPHY

Bly, R. & Booth, W. (Ed.) (1992). A Little Book on the Human Shadow. Harper San Francisco.

Bly, R. & Woodman, M. (1999). The Maiden King: The Reunion of Masculine and Feminine. Owl Books.

Campbell, J. (1962). The Hero with a Thousand Faces. The World Publishing Company.

Estes, C.P. (2005). Warming the Stone Child: Myths and Stories about Abandonment and the Unmothered Child. Sounds True (unabridged audiobook).

Jung, C.G. (2001). Essays on a Science of Mythology. Princeton University Press.

Jung, C.G. (2005). Science of Mythology: Essays on the Myth of the Divine Child and the Mysteries of Eleusis. Routledge.

Matthews, J. (2002). At the Table of the Grail: No One Who Sets Forth on the Grail Quest Remains Unchanged. Watkins Publishing, Ltd.

Moore, T. (1994). Care of the Soul: A Guide for Cultivating Depth and Sacredness in Everyday Life. Harper Paperbacks.

Zweig, C. & Abrams, J. (1991). Meeting the Shadow: The Hidden Power of the Dark Side of Human Nature. J.P. Tarcher.

Printed in the United States
102217LV00001B/1-99/A

9 781595 941312